Penikese Island Adventure

Written by Kathleen Hickey

Edited by Michael Mattes

Briley & Baxter Publications | Plymouth, Massachusetts

ISBN: 978-1-954819-05-4

Book Design: Stacy O'Halloran

Dedicated to my mother, Mary, who instilled in me the love of reading

Preface

To my readers,

For several years, my husband and I passed by the seemingly deserted island of Penikese, while motoring to Cuttyhunk Island off the coast of Massachusetts. Curious about it, I decided to conduct some research. What I found was fascinating!

From a one-time scientific research center to the current day wildlife sanctuary, the island has been the home of several ventures over the years. I was lucky enough to finally visit the island for a day on a scheduled Audubon Society tour, and that motivated me to develop my story and share the beauty and history of this island.

In the early 1900's, the first and only leprosarium in Massachusetts was located on Penikese Island. Fifty years later, in the 1970's, a school for delinquent youths was started on the island. It was this "camp," as it was referred to, that started me thinking about the storyline I would pursue.

What if the person who started this school decided to bring his daughter along for the summer? Placing the story in current time, I tell the story of Julia, an only child from a privileged but estranged family. Julia lives with her mother in Connecticut during the school year but spends time with her father every summer, usually in New York City, where he lives. This summer, however, she reluctantly travels to the isolated island of Penikese with her father and his team—that's where the adventure begins.

Sincerely,
Kathleen Hickey

Chapter 1

Diego went out to gather more sticks for the fire while I divvied up the food; it was not much, but it would have to do. Diego came back with the fuel supplies, and after adding them to the stove, he ate up his portion of the food. Jake lay down closest to the stove, and Franklin took his blanket and settled in one of the far corners. That left one thin sheet on the cot and a grubby looking pillow. Diego insisted that I take the cot, and he settled on the floor not far from the stove.

Discarding the pillow on the floor, I lay down and tried to get comfortable. I was worried sick about what would happen when we got back and wished I had mentioned to Dad where I was heading. I could not imagine what he thought when none of us showed up for dinner, and I was sure that there was a search party out there looking for us by now. *This is not going to end well,* I thought as I nodded off to sleep.

I woke up a few hours later, shivering and confused as to where I was. I sat up frightened when I heard something or someone stirring near me. "It's just me, Julia," Diego whispered. "I figured you may be getting cold, so I brought this to cover you." Diego slipped his flannel shirt over me, and I settled back in the bed, already somehow warmer.

"What about you? You must be freezing," I said quietly.

"I'm fine," he answered. "I just put some more wood on the fire. Try to get a little more sleep. The storm is passing quickly. We'll have to be leaving soon."

"I'm worried about my dad. He must be frantic worrying about me... about all of us. The whole crew must have been out all night looking for us."

"I went out a few times to see if I could hear them or see them," Diego responded. "I didn't hear anything. We'll head back in a couple of hours when I can make out the path."

I lay back down, warmer than before and tried to sleep again. As I dozed off, I wondered again how this efficient, mature boy could have ended up out here as a delinquent.

* * *

Two Weeks Prior

"I'm not going... I don't have to go. I just got here, and you're making me go away before I even settle in!" I was practicing my speech that I would deliver to my dad when he got home from work that night.

Having just arrived from my mom's house in Connecticut the weekend before—after spending the previous school year with her—I was looking forward to spending the summer with Dad in New York City. I was especially excited now that I was finally "old enough" to explore the city on my own. My parents had made this arrangement three years before when they "amicably" decided to separate and live apart. Dad hadn't been around much before that anyway; I had reasoned at the time. Still, the nights in our big house in New Canaan, Connecticut felt a lot quieter and lonelier after he left.

"Julia, are you packed yet?" Dad asked as he half-knocked and walked into my bedroom, looking apprehensive and surprisingly young.

"Dad, tell me again where we are going this summer and why we have to go?"

"Julia, I explained all of this to you last week. I've been working on this project all year, and the opportunity came up just recently to put my plan into practice on the island of Penikese, just off the coast of Massachusetts. It's a great opportunity for both of us to be together and have some private time exploring a new area."

2

I knew my father was excited about starting this summer camp where he would be the head psychologist working with a group of troubled boys from the area around the city. He had been working with the boys over the past year and knew that, for some of them, this was their last chance for redemption before entering into the juvenile justice system that he was so against. All my arguments disappeared as I looked at his anxious face; I realized that I could not take this opportunity away from him.

"Do you want me to go back and spend the summer with Mom? It would probably make things so much easier for you if I did," I asked timidly, not sure how I wanted him to answer.

"Definitely not… unless you want to, honey? I think it will be fun and interesting for you, and I'm sure you would be helpful if you came."

How could I possibly be helpful at a camp with twelve troubled boys and several trained staff members out on an island in the middle of nowhere? He had explained to me that some of the boys were recovering from substance abuse, so the staff would consist of himself, three other counselors, three interns, two maintenance workers, a nurse, and a cook. Somehow, though, I did suspect that it would be an adventure and something I could write about for my junior year writing course. I was really looking forward to that class, and I was super psyched that I got into the AP level course a year early. My goal was to be the top student in the 2018 graduating class, and this essay class would go far in helping me achieve this goal.

"Almost packed, Dad," I simply replied.

I knew my mom would miss me, but she was also planning on spending the whole summer researching and preparing her final dissertation for her master's degree in art history from Yale University. She had been working so hard to complete her workload along with having a full-time job and plotting out time for me. She almost seemed relieved when I was finally ready to leave for the summer.

The next morning, Dad and I took a plane to Greene Airport in Rhode Island and then rented a car before heading to Woods Hole, Massachusetts. Unfortunately, we then missed the connecting ferry to our next destination, so we went to a bed and breakfast that my mother had suggested to Dad when she heard we were running behind schedule.

After a light dinner of burgers and fries, Dad suggested we "hit the sack" in order to get up early and make the first ferry out in the morning. Tired—but a bit excited as well—I fell asleep wondering what tomorrow would bring.

It was windy and rainy when the ferry dropped us off. There were several people on the ferry, but I should have been suspicious when only Dad and I got off the boat amongst the waves and gusty winds. Upon my first observation of the island, I was shocked to see a big, flat space covered with low-growing bushes and not much else. When I looked closer, I could see a few low buildings in the distance. Dad was so excited that I tried not to let my skeptical mood get him down. Two men dressed in foul-weather gear met us at the dock. We introduced ourselves to the two workers as they loaded our belongings into a motorized, open vehicle and drove us to the camp.

It was a bumpy ride along a worn-down path up a slight incline to the school where we would spend the rest of the summer. Only three other counselors, along with the nurse and cook, had arrived the day before, according to one of the men. The buildings were low and seemed to be made from wood. Inside the main building, it was warm and smelled like fresh paint. The walls were all pale yellow and green, and it felt like they were trying too hard to be cheerful. I made a mental note to remember that thought when I ultimately started my essay about this experience. Dad seemed anxious to meet up with the staff who were there. After dumping my supplies in our living quarters, I decided to do some exploring of my own.

There appeared to be only three buildings on the property: one dorm-type building where we would sleep; one school-type building with classrooms, a kitchen, and a cafeteria; and a third building that looked like an old fishing shack. The dorm where I would be living had two floors. Dad and I, the nurse, and the cook would be on the bottom floor, and the boys as well as the rest of the staff would be on the second.

The fishing shack interested me the most, as it looked like a possible project for me to get involved in. It was full of supplies for outdoor activities like fishing, kayaking, and sailing, and it also had many materials that could be used for craft projects. I felt comfortable in the big, unkept space with open shelves and cabinets filled with adventures and projects waiting to happen. This building seemed warmer than the others as well. This was perhaps because, upon closer inspection, I realized it was built of stone and rocks with large windows that let in a lot of light. Later, I learned that it was the only existing building leftover from a natural history laboratory that was established on this island in the 1870's.

Dad caught up with me an hour later while I was sorting through some craft supplies that had been piled in one of the open bins. I explained to him that this is where I would like to volunteer, and he promised to pass the idea on to the counselor who would be supervising the shed and outdoor activities. After heading back to the main building, Dad introduced me to the staff who were present. Everyone seemed as equally excited as Dad and obviously looked up to him. I met the three counselors who would be working with the boys as well as the nurse, Ann, and Maria, the cook. Dad explained that the three interns would be coming the next day on the ferry with the boys.

I decided to help with lunch while they all talked. I immediately bonded with Maria, who seemed fun and motherly—though she was nothing like my sophisticated mother at home. Lunch consisted of sandwiches and fruit that we put on metal plates. This was going to be much more like camping than I originally expected. Maria explained to me that the food supplies would be dropped off once a week by a passing ferry, depending on the weather conditions.

I was exhausted by the time lunch was over but still volunteered to help Maria with the cleanup. Afterward, I went back to my room and fell asleep on my bunk to the sound of waves crashing on the shore, which helped me to sleep soundly for a couple of hours.

I woke up startled, confused at first as to where I was. I got up and wandered around the compound not sure what to do with myself. I remembered how comfortable I felt with Maria, so I went back to the kitchen and found her organizing shelves and storing products that had been dropped off earlier. I offered to help, and she seemed happy with the offer. We worked together until she had to start planning dinner. I felt like we had just eaten, but I again offered to help her with the food preparation, and the time passed quickly as she taught me how to make a stew from the ingredients we had just unpacked. By the time it was ready, I was quite hungry again and could not wait to sit down and enjoy a meal with Dad. I put plates of bread and butter on the table along with silverware and napkins. I was relieved that we were not using plastic utensils for this great stew.

Everyone seemed to enjoy the stew and talked excitedly about the upcoming project. I felt a little out of the loop, and I hoped that Dad and I could have some private time to talk about everything together. But he seemed so happy and close to these people that I did not want to seem moody, so I tried to sit and eat in a contented-looking silence. It apparently worked, as Dad kept looking over at me and giving me a thumbs-up.

After dinner, I helped clean up, which went amazingly fast since everyone pitched in and brought their own plates into the kitchen. By the time the kitchen was cleaned and sorted, I could not believe how tired I was once again. I said goodnight to Dad, who was conversing quietly with his staff, and headed back to the dorm. On my way, I noticed the most beautiful sunset I had ever seen in my life while looking out to the western part of the island. I made a mental note to visually memorize this picture in my brain and went back to my room to write down the feeling I was experiencing in my notes. After finishing my journal entry, I decided to go to bed much earlier than I had in a long time.

Chapter 2

The birds woke me up before the sun did. I descended from my top bunk, enjoying the novelty of it all; I've always wanted to sleep on a top bunk, but being an only child, I never had the opportunity. Dad had offered me one of the single rooms on this floor, but after looking out of the big window in the bunkroom, I was glad for the choice I made. From the window, I could see and smell the ocean in the distance, and I could even hear the sea birds squawking away.

On the way to breakfast, I ran into Ann. I noticed she had a yoga mat with her, so I asked her about it. Apparently, yoga was her passion, and she would be running classes on the beach twice a week all summer. She hoped to entice the rest of the staff, and even some of the boys, to join her throughout the summer. Declining her invitation for me to join her, I told her that I would keep it in mind for another time. We talked for a few minutes more, and I learned that she currently lived in New York but had grown up here in Massachusetts. She had visited many of the islands around the state, but she had never been on this island. She raved about Dad and what an opportunity it was for her to work with him. She had a sparkle in her eye when mentioning Dad, and I wondered about that as I walked into breakfast. He was a handsome man, and I would not have a problem with him being involved with someone other than my mom again... would I?

Breakfast was delicious; Maria had prepared us all hot oatmeal that tasted wonderful with brown sugar and raisins on top. Searching for Dad after I was done eating, I found him with the other counselors who were helping to unload a supply boat that had just arrived. Standing off to one side were a group of tired looking boys, most of them frowning and looking extremely bored and angry. One taller boy did come forward and helped Dad as he struggled to unload a larger-than-normal trunk off the boat. As I approached Dad, one of the heavier boys looked me over and did a small wolf whistle. He was pushing it for sure; I hardly looked like a girl at all while dressed in my sweats, boots, oversized jacket, and hat that covered all my "dirty" blond hair. My friends and I had experimented with our hair at the end of the school year, much to my mother's dismay. "Why would you take your lovely, light brown hair and put that nasty color in it?" she had questioned. After that, I "loved" my look, and I told her that it was just what I was going for. It was a bit grown out now, though, and I wondered how I was going to continue that look here.

Dad walked over to the group of boys with one of the other counselors and talked to them in a low voice for a short time. The larger boy walked closer to me and mumbled something that sounded like an insincere apology, and I just nodded my head in response. The boys then headed up to the main building for breakfast, and I followed behind with Dad as the others drove the motorized cart to the dormitory to unload.

Dad explained to me that only ten boys had made it to the island, as two of them had added infractions to their offenses that made them ineligible for the trip. I could tell that Dad was upset about this, as he took each of these boys and his project much to heart. Trying to cheer him up, I pointed out that it would give him more time to spend with the boys who did come, but that did not seem to help much. He wanted me to follow him to the cafeteria to meet the boys, but I begged off by saying I'm sure they needed time to settle in by themselves before being overwhelmed with introductions.

Not sure what to do next, I walked back to the fishing shack and again began organizing the craft section as best I could. I had been introduced to Dan, the counselor who would oversee this area, the night before at dinner. He seemed happy for me to volunteer with him and gave me permission to organize any area I felt needed it. I got the impression that each of these young counselors were somewhat overwhelmed with their multiple assignments and needed help wherever it was offered.

The place was cluttered and dirty but did have a warm, welcoming feeling about it. Checking out all the drawers and cabinets was fun, with treasures appearing in every reveal. After working for about two hours, I decided to take a water break and eat the fruit bar that Maria had given me after breakfast. I had just sat down on one of the benches when I heard someone entering the building. Thinking it was probably Dan, I got up to greet him when suddenly I realized it was one of the boys from this morning. I recognized him as the taller boy who had stepped up to help Dad with the heavy trunk.

Neither of us said anything at first, but eventually he said, "Sorry" and started to walk out.

"Wait," I said, "you can stay and look around. I'm Julia, and I help out here." I did not want to advertise that I was the headmaster's daughter, though it was probably obvious when Dad had hugged me as we walked up the path after the unloading.

He hesitated for a minute and then said, "I'm Diego." He was tall and thin with very dark hair—a bit longer than I was used to on the boys I knew back home. As he walked a bit closer, I noticed his eyes were also very dark and sad looking. He did not shy away, however, and kept his eyes on mine until I finally looked away.

"This is the project area for the craft and outdoor activities. I was just trying to straighten it out a bit," I explained.

"They said we could look around on our own," he said. "Most of the guys just went back to nap, but I wanted to do a little exploring. This building is cool. The others feel like a juvie hall." Looking embarrassed at that remark, he quickly added, "I've never been in one, though... except to visit my brother." After a moment longer, he said, "I'll see you later maybe; you look like you have a lot to do here."

My heart did that little flip thing it does when I meet a cute guy. *Hmmm*, I thought, *maybe I will have something to write my best friend, Meg, about this summer.* Remembering that this summer was supposed to be about writing an interesting, exciting essay for college entry, though, I pushed that thought out of my mind and got busy again with my organizing.

At lunch, I was introduced to the rest of the boys, most of whom either muttered a quick, shy "hello" or just nodded their heads. When Dad came to Diego, he also just nodded his head but did give me more eye contact than the others. Dad explained to the boys that they would have the rest of the day free to explore but that organized activities would start the next day and their schedules would be on the bulletin board in the front hall.

Curious about their "activities," I questioned Dad about what that entailed. He listed for me what their day-to-day agenda would be like: breakfast; meds (when necessary); group and individual counseling; work shifts; lunch; free time; more scheduled activities (indoor or outdoor); free time; supper; group meetings; and then bed. He did add that the boys were welcomed to go fishing whenever they had time and how great early-morning fishing was. Also, he mentioned the yoga sessions that Ann would be offering a couple of mornings a week. I wondered how much Dad really understood about teenage boys if he thought they would give up their sleep for those things, but I did not interject.

The whole schedule sounded so regimented to me, but then Dad reminded me of what their alternative would have been. I tried to get him to tell me what some of their infractions were, but he would not elaborate on those. I asked him about weekends and if their schedules would be the same then. He explained that they would have time off on weekends to email family, sleep more, and wander about a bit. Apparently, this island was "pretty" secure and quite far away from other land areas.

After lunch, I decided to explore some of the island on my own once again. I had little fear of getting lost, as this part of the island was mostly open, and it appeared you could see our buildings from most of the spots surrounding us. It was a warm day, but I dressed well-covered to prevent mosquito and tick bites. There were paths leading in all directions from our small compound, so I decided to take the northern one. Having a good sense of direction from my girl scout days, I headed off confidently with a feeling of freedom—I even had the compass my mom had bought me as a reward for selling so many girl scout cookies when I was a kid. Maybe I wasn't exploring the big city, but I was an explorer on an isolated island.

The path led down an incline, and it became apparent that it was leading right to the ocean. Small flowers and shrubs lined the path along with many bushes of berries that I would have to research when I got back to my room. My mom had given me a set of nature books on birds and ground coverings of this area. I would add what I learned to my daily journal and perhaps also inject it into my essay somehow.

Slowly the path became steeper and rockier. When I reached the beach, I was amazed at the beauty of what I saw. The water was rougher than what I was used to, but it was so beautiful with the sun reflecting on it. In the distance, I could see the mainland and even make out some of the huge mansions that lined the opposite shore. There were so many different varieties of birds that I'd need to research once I got back to my room as well.

As I turned to walk up the shoreline, I noticed someone sitting on a rock not far away. I could tell from my quickened heartbeat and the color of his hair just who it was. Not wanting to disturb him, I told myself to turn and go the other way. However, my feet did not listen to this reasoning, and before I knew it, I was just a few feet away from Diego. He didn't seem to notice me, and he was leaning back against another rock. His eyes were also closed, and I began to wonder if he was asleep. I tried to think of something witty to say, but nothing came to mind, so I started to back away. As I did, he said, "You can sit if you want."

"You look like you don't want company. I don't want to bother you when you're resting," I replied.

"Up to you."

"It's gorgeous here, isn't it? So peaceful," I asked.

"I've never seen the ocean this close before," he said quietly. "Some people get to wake up and see this every day. One day, that will be me."

Perhaps it was nervous talking, but I just started asking him all about himself. Specifically, I asked what grade he was in and if he had any other siblings besides his brother. He said he was entering his senior year in high school and lived with his dad, stepmother, and stepbrother in the Bronx area of New York.

I explained that I lived with my mom in Connecticut and had no siblings. I was spending the summer here on the island with Dad, helping him out. He snickered a little when I said that, but I chose to ignore him.

"I'm surprised he let you come here and be around all of us delinquents," he said sarcastically.

"Dad doesn't think like that at all," I said in response, "and I assure you that I'm old enough to take care of myself and do my job."

"Yeah, Dr. Cooper's a decent guy," he said, "but I'm just not sure what I'm doing here when I should be home helping my stepmom."

I did not know what to say to that, so I just stared at the ocean. After a few minutes of silence, I decided to go. As I was getting up, he said, "I have Saturday morning off, so I was thinking of exploring the western trail then."

I walked back to my dorm room quickly wondering why that would matter to me.

Chapter 3

The next few days went by quickly. I started working with Dan in the fishing shack, organizing and setting up indoor and outdoor projects. He had the expertise and know-how, but he listened when I made a few suggestions. For example, somehow, I did not think these ten boys would be interested in making bead bracelets, even for their girlfriends or moms. I suggested that we should instead teach them how to make rope bracelets, which they could use for themselves or whomever they chose to give them to. He agreed to that and a few other suggestions I made for the indoor activities.

We cleaned and separated the supplies for fishing, kayaking, canoeing, and sailing. We had an abundance of rope, so we decided to make a rope obstacle course outside. This was a challenge, however, since there were no tall trees to attach the ropes to. Instead, we decided to use the boards we found out back to make structures to attach the ropes to. This was a bit too much work for the two of us alone, so we asked the boys to volunteer to help us.

Only three boys showed up to help during their free time: a smaller boy named Jake, the bigger boy who had whistled at me earlier (whose name is Franklin), and, of course, Diego. It turns out that Diego had natural carpentry skills, which helped us finish the project in no time at all. He seemed to also have leadership skills and oversaw the other boys easily. Dan, who seemed to be aware of his skills, let him do his thing but also kept a careful eye on him throughout the project. I wondered at the time why all the scrutiny but brushed it off as being conscientious with the boys.

We worked on the rope course in our free time for the rest of the week. It was a simple course, but we needed to make sure that it was secure and safe. After a while, Dan stopped coming out of the shed to help us, but he never took his eyes off what we were doing. The boys and I started to form some great camaraderie as the week passed.

On the way back to the dorm after one successful morning of construction, I complimented Diego on his building skills. He responded by saying, "I hope to be a contractor one day or maybe even an engineer." Dan, who was not far behind us but also close enough to hear our conversation, snickered at that comment. I thought about mentioning his attitude to Dad, but I decided to wait and see if it improved. He certainly did not seem to fit the model of acceptance that Dad was obviously going for here at the camp.

On Saturday morning, I got up early, not quite sure what time I would go exploring the western trail. I ate breakfast quickly and headed out on my own, with no expectations— none whatsoever. The morning was cooler, and it was misting a bit, so I wore my rain jacket over my sweatshirt. I did take some time to fix my hair, though. It was smooth and straight when I left the dorm, but now I could tell it was curling up on its way to a major frizz. *Oh well*, I thought as I threw on my baseball cap and headed up the western path.

As I was walking, I started to notice small shells on the path every few steps. *Curious*, I thought, *I hadn't noticed this before on the other paths.* As I walked further, I also noticed several offshoots from the main path, some of them the same width of the path itself, but I continued to stay on the trail with the shells. When I came to a fork in the path, the shells continued toward the right, but there were none on the left. I followed the path on the right until I came to a small graveyard overlooking the ocean. I was shocked to see it there, and I stood still looking around at the scene. Suddenly, I heard a rustling noise behind me.

"These graves are old," Diego said. "The ones I could still read go back to the early 1900s. Most of the stones are broken down or nonexistent, but there are grave markers in their place. I counted fourteen altogether. One belonged to a little child born in 1917 and died in 1918."

"That's weird," I said. "I didn't think anyone ever lived here for an extended time. I'll have to ask Dad about this place and do some research. This will be great to add to my paper."

"Paper?" he asked.

"I'm taking a senior research course in the fall. You spend the whole term working on a research paper, which can then be used for a college entry essay. That's the main reason I decided to come here this summer—that and the chance to hang out with Dad."

"Don't you see him much?"

"No, not really. I see him when I come to New York, but I don't get that opportunity very often. He doesn't have the time to see me in Connecticut more than once a year. You live with both your parents?"

"Dad's in prison. My mom died when I was young. My stepmom is pretty cool, though."

"Oh… I'm sorry," was all I could say. I wanted to say more but did not know exactly what.

The graveyard was sitting at a perfect spot overlooking the open ocean, and I hoped it was put there on purpose. After looking around for a while at the graves and admiring where they were situated, we walked down a little incline toward some other markers in the distance. We came to a clearing off the path with several stone posts sticking out of the ground. There seemed to have been a little village here at one time, which piqued my curiosity even more.

The sun was finally above us and it was starting to get quite warm. I took off my rain jacket and stuffed it in my backpack. I then unpacked some snack bars, and two water bottles I had in there as well and offered them to Diego. He took one of each and sat down on one of the stones we had discovered.

"Nice touch with the shells," I said.

He just smiled but didn't say anything. I wanted to ask him what his dad had done and, more so, what he had done to end up here on the island, but I did not know how to start. He seemed to sense my awkwardness and said, "Dad is not a bad person. He got caught up with the wrong guys and was involved with a robbery where someone got hurt."

I waited to see if he was going to say anything more. When he did not, I asked, "How long has he been there?"

"For about a year, but he comes up for a review in a couple of months. I'm hoping they can shorten his sentence then. I plan to be there with my stepmom. Your dad said he would go with us also. He's quite a guy, your dad."

I didn't reply; I just smiled, realizing how lucky I really was to have my two parents. We finished our snack and then walked back to the compound together in silence. I was anxious to talk to Dad and do some research on my own about this island. It now seemed to hold some stories that I intended to unearth.

After talking to Dad and Ann—it turns out she knew a lot more about the history of this island than Dad—I headed to my computer to do some research. Ann filled me in on many of the details, but she was unclear on the exact dates involved. Through talking to her as well as my own research, I learned that this island had been the site of a hospital and special village for lepers starting in the year 1905. The "experiment," as it was referred to, lasted for several years before it was closed. The graveyard Diego and I found held the bodies of the patients who had died here, and the stone posts must have been the remnants of their cottages, or perhaps the hospital itself. My research further uncovered some brave heroics from the medical staff here at that time as well as several sad stories about the families that were separated for years without any contact or knowledge about their loved ones. This would most definitely fit into my essay, but somehow, I was more excited about talking to Diego about what I had discovered.

I wondered what Diego's plans were for the next day since Sundays were mostly free for the boys. Dad had me "pencil in" some time for him the next afternoon since he had been too busy to spend much time with me. He mentioned the possibility of heading back to the leper colony site so I could show him what I found. I was hoping I could meet up with Diego before that and fill him in on what I had learned.

My dilemma was solved when I walked into the cafeteria and saw him helping Maria in the kitchen. I learned that the boys could make extra spending money to use in the small store set up outside the kitchen by helping with certain jobs. He passed me a note as I picked up my tray for food. My heart did that little flip thing again, and I felt like I was back in junior high.

The note read: "Meet me tomorrow morning around 7ish on the northern trail again. I found out some interesting news I want to share with you."

Chapter 4

The next morning, Diego and I began our walk after an early breakfast. It was a cool, crisp morning, and it felt good to sit, eat, and just hang out with someone who felt like a friend. It was the first time we had planned to do something together, having always just "run into" each other before.

As we headed down the western path, Diego started telling me about some research he conducted on the colony we discovered. I felt a bit disappointed at first; he was giving me facts about the leper colony in much more detail than I had gathered from my research. Snapping out of my mood, I proceeded to tell him that I had found similar information and had also talked to Ann about the area. We continued to compare notes all the way back to the cemetery. Looking over the worn-down graves, this time with new knowledge, made me feel even more attached to the people who were buried there. I wondered if Diego felt the same, but when I turned around and looked at his face, I knew he did.

Proceeding up the incline together to the stone enclosures, we tried to picture what everything was like back then. We figured that the largest stones, which were also the furthest apart, must have been remnants of the small hospital, and the other stones perhaps marked the little cottages for the inhabitants and hospital staff. We had both learned in our research that the leprosarium had been vacated in 1921, and shortly after that all the buildings were burnt down. We continued to discuss what we knew from our research and what we knew about leprosy in general. Once again, I was surprised by his knowledge; I guess I had assumed I was a more advanced reader than he was—but it seemed I was wrong.

Seeing the surprise on my face, he said, "There's not much for me to do in the city to keep busy, so I spend a lot of time at our local library. My stepmom works two jobs, so rather than stay home alone, I walked to the library when I was younger. Now I have a job after school, but I still go and check out books often." When I didn't say anything in response, he added, "You're wondering how I ended up out here, aren't you?"

"No... yes... maybe?" I answered, embarrassed by the change in conversation and for having my thoughts read so clearly. "I mean, you seem so normal to be here with these other guys."

"Your dad hasn't told you about my life?" he asked.

"No," I answered, "he would never share anything that has to do with his boys or his job like that."

Diego thought about that a moment and said, "Yeah, I guess I can't picture Dr. Cooper sharing any of our details. He's an OK guy... for a counselor. There's not much of a story really. I looked up to Dad, and he ended up in prison. Then I hung out with my stepbrother and got caught up in some things I shouldn't have. When he almost ended up in juvenile detention, I decided to get my act together and look for a job after school. I'm here because, right before that, my stepbrother asked me to help him out with 'one last thing'—and then he promised he was done. Stupidly, I went along with him, and we were caught. Luckily, instead of sending me to juvie court because of my age and lack of a record, I got referred to your dad. Dr. C appeased the courts by telling them about his new program and assuring them I would participate. So, here I am for the summer. I really should be back in New York, however, making some money to help my stepmom. Our rent is crazy, and now she is on her own handling everything herself."

I was impressed by his dedication to her, but not knowing what else to say I suggested that we start walking back to the compound. We were quiet on the way back, but I noticed we walked a little closer together than before, and I felt a warm friendship starting, which surprised me. Normally, my friends were all girls, and my crushes were boys who I barely knew. I did have a "boyfriend" last year, who I met at dances and walked around the school halls with before class, but we never really had a serious discussion like the one I just had with Diego.

When I told my then-boyfriend, Craig, that I was going away for the whole summer, he did not seem upset and only said, "That's fine… I figured it was time that we start dating others anyway." Since that did not hurt me very much, Meg suggested that I really was not "in love" with him anyway, so good riddance.

When we got back to the compound, Diego said he was going to be busy for the next few days but wanted to explore the southern part of the island the following Saturday.

"Sounds like a plan," I said happily before heading to the main building for a lunch date with Dad, who was waiting for me in the cafeteria sipping a cup of coffee.

"Hi, Hun. Where have you been?" he asked.

"I went back to the leper colony again to check it out."

"By yourself?"

Hmm, I thought, *he's fishing for some information.* "No, actually, I went with a friend."

"You've made a friend here?"

"Yes, I ran into Diego and we walked up together," I said casually.

"That was a fast friendship. We just got here a short time ago. He's a nice fellow, but I wouldn't get too close to him."

"Why not?"

"Well, Hun, he is a student here, and they have certain restrictions and rules they have to live under. And besides that, he's a bit older and more worldly than you."

"I thought you wanted them to feel as normal as possible here. Is there a rule I don't know about that they can't make friends with anyone but the other inmates?"

"First of all, Julia, they are not 'inmates,' as you well know. Second, there is no rule like that. We just don't want him to be on the outs with the other boys. If they are jealous of him, they won't bond or share with him, and that's part of the program also."

"It's no big deal, Dad, we just talked a few times. Don't worry about it."

After lunch, I told Dad I had to write a few emails and was too tired to go for our walk together. He seemed a bit disappointed but just nodded. I was not as carefree as I was when I entered the building for lunch, and as I left, I wondered if Dad would say something to Diego. I wished I had asked him to stay out of it altogether, but I've learned the hard way that asking such things is a sure way to make a parent become more involved than ever.

I went back to the dorm to write to my friend Meg and my mom. Our computers and phones had limited internet connection here, so it seemed like forever to get a note sent out. My letter to my mom just outlined my days here and gave her some of the details I had learned about the leper colony. I told her I was enjoying myself and what I was staying busy doing. I asked how her research was going and what she was doing for fun. I was hoping she was getting out a bit with her friends and relaxing somewhat.

I had been excited to write to Meg and share my news about Diego, but after talking to Dad, I was not so sure. If he made a big deal of our friendship and forced Diego to stop talking to me, there would be nothing to tell Meg in the future and she might think I was making the whole thing up in my head… again. Just a few months ago, I was sure Craig was going to ask me to be exclusive, so I called Meg all excited.

When we did meet up for our movie date, though, his "big news" was only that he made the all-star baseball team for the upcoming summer. Meg's comment was that I had to learn to "read boys" better and realize that they are all the same—only thinking about themselves all the time and no one else. I decided I would wait to tell Meg about Diego another time, if at all.

Chapter 5

Waking up to another beautiful morning, I decided to try Ann's yoga class. As I walked by, I noticed Dad was already up and fishing with two of the boys down at the small dock. Who knew he enjoyed that sport? I pretended not to see him as I walked the path to the beach area and laid my towel down near Ann, who was obviously meditating. She smiled when she looked up and said she would be done in a moment.

I enjoyed just listening to the seagulls and looking out at the ocean all around us. One other person joined us as we were just beginning our morning warmups. It was one of the interns I had met earlier named Matt. He was a student from NYU, who, like the others, was super excited about being involved with Dad's program. The exercise was harder than I thought. I started out assuming that I would be the star, but I quickly learned that I was far less coordinated than I believed. During our "cool down," I looked around and was surprised to see that Ann and Matt looked a lot less glimmery than me.

After our session, I walked back to the main building for breakfast and sat down with Ann and Matt. Some of the boys were starting to drift in, but Dad and the two he was fishing with were still out on the dock. I wondered who the boys were since I could not tell from where the path turned. Hmmm… one of them did look just like Diego. I had decided that maybe I should take some coffee and drinks down to them when Dad walked in. He smiled at me, and I noticed he gave a special smile to Ann also.

Walking behind Dad were Diego and Jake, who both went to sit at a small table by themselves even though Dad tried to invite them to sit down with us. Diego did not give me any eye contact, and I wondered what that was about. Dad came over and joined us just as I was getting up to help Maria with cleaning.

"How was yoga?" he asked.

"Fine," I answered. "How was fishing?"

"Very good actually. The boys each caught three stripers, and I caught two. I'm going to teach them how to clean them after breakfast and then give them to Maria for supper tonight."

I wanted to ask him what they talked about, but I knew he would not share that information, so I just nodded and walked into the kitchen to help Maria. She was staring at the bucket of fish, looking perplexed.

"Dad said he and the boys are going to clean those later, Maria," I told her quickly.

"You better believe they are," she responded with a wink.

"How did you end up here, Maria?" I asked. "Did you know Dad from New York?"

"Yes," she answered. "He has helped my family a lot over the last few years. My son, Luis, became involved with a gang in our neighborhood, and I couldn't afford to move out of the area. My husband had died a few years earlier, and Luis never really got over that. The courts had mandated that Luis meet with Dr. Cooper for a few sessions after he was involved in a fight with another gang. He continued to see him over the next year, even after the mandated hours. I could not afford to pay him, so I cooked for him and brought dinner to the sessions each week."

"Where's Luis now?" I asked.

"That was a couple of years ago. Luis completely turned his life around. He got a good job working construction and moved in with his girlfriend in another neighborhood. They are expecting a little one in the fall. I'm working on them to get married, but young couples don't seem to rush into that these days," she added with a smirk.

"So, you decided to come here to help Dad?"

"Even though he no longer sees Luis, I still bring him food now and then. On one visit, he shared with me his vision, and when I offered to come help, he hired me on the spot. I was excited to come and get out of the heat of the city and visit an island for the first time in my life."

"Yes, his enthusiasm is hard to resist," I added, "and you can't beat the atmosphere around here for working conditions."

I was beginning to see how much Dad has done—and has continued doing—for others and how important his work here is. I wanted to seek him out and see if we could take that walk, I had promised him earlier. However, I knew he would be busy for the rest of the morning, so I went back to my room to work on my paper.

The next afternoon, we finally got to go out for our walk together. We walked at a relaxed pace, as it was an especially hot and muggy day. He seemed relaxed and happy as we headed up the trail.

"Dad," I began, "I'm really proud of the work you're doing here and the work you have been doing in New York these past few years. It couldn't have been easy being all by yourself."

"Thanks, Julia," he responded. "My staff and my patients help me to feel accepted and needed. And I really love what I do, though at times it is extremely hard. But I do hate being so far away from you."

"I feel the same way, Dad," I said, and then added, "but at least you have Ann there in the city."

"Ann?" he questioned, a bit too quickly.

"Dad, I'm not an idiot," I answered. "I really like her, and I think it's great if you guys are more than just friends."

"It's pretty new, Julia. That's why I hadn't mentioned her to you. And I haven't had a chance to let your mom know either, so I would prefer that you didn't mention it to her," he said pleadingly.

"How did you guys meet?" I asked.

"She works in the rehab hospital where some of my patients go for detox. She's been wonderful," he added. "She believes, like I do, that many of these boys just need more understanding and a second chance. When I told her about my summer program, she asked to join the team and I was thrilled to have her."

"I can understand why, Dad," I said. "And she is pretty cute."

He tried pushing me off the trail as I ran ahead of him laughing, and we proceeded comfortably toward the graveyard.

When we got there, we spent a few moments in silence, and I could tell he was as affected by it as Diego and I were when we first saw it.

After a while we visited the colony site and then worked our way back to the compound in silence, both lost in our thoughts of what we had seen and what we had discussed earlier.

I wanted to bring up Diego again and how nice it was to have him here to share what I was feeling. I thought maybe Dad would understand now if I compared it to his feelings for Ann. But I decided against it. Somehow, I did not want anything to affect the nice afternoon we had just shared together.

Chapter 6

The next few days went by quickly, and I stayed quite busy. Dan started his outdoor classes, many of which I participated in; I figured I could get to know the rest of the boys better if I learned along with them. Some were more athletic than others in learning the new sports, and, of course, Diego was right up there with the best. I struggled to keep up with the lower half, but I held my own and helped where I could.

Each day, we were introduced to a new outdoor sport—either fishing, sailing, kayaking, or canoeing. I had done some kayaking with my mom before, so that was my favorite. Slowly, I got to know the boys better and earned some of their respect... especially when I landed in the water, repeatedly, without complaining. Surprisingly, I became a bit closer to Franklin, who had to help me get out of the water and back in the boat more than once. I continued to be perplexed by Dan's treatment of Diego, who always seemed helpful and respectful toward Dan. Dan was short with him, always criticizing him more than the others. After one session when I stayed after to help Dan clean up, I asked him about it.

"Don't know what you're talking about, Julia," he responded to me. "I treat all the guys here the same. I think you're a bit sensitive to Diego, though, probably because you have an obvious crush on him."

I was uncomfortable with his response and debated talking to my dad about it, but I decided not to intervene. After all, he was one of Dad's choices as counselor, so I had to trust his decision.

Three of the boys could not participate in any of the water sports because they could not swim. Since I had my lifeguarding certificate, I volunteered to help them learn. It was a challenge in the ocean, however, as I was used to teaching in a community pool. Diego volunteered to help me when he could; he was also a strong swimmer, having spent many years in the Boy's Club pool in his neighborhood back home. Again, I was overcome with how different he was than the other boys here. He seemed so normal and much more adjusted than the other guys, and they seemed to respect him more and more.

To fit these sessions into their schedule, we had to meet early in the morning twice a week. The water was quite cold here, and the fog often hadn't lifted this early in the morning. I chose to teach on Tuesdays and Thursdays so I would not interfere with Ann's yoga classes, which I was enjoying more and more each time I went. I also liked the opportunity to get to know her better, especially if she was going to be in Dad's life.

On Thursday morning, I headed down to the shore with my towel and backpack. I arrived a bit earlier than the boys, so I started putting out the floats and other devices I planned to use that morning. I heard a rustling sound and turned around. Diego was standing there with his towel, just staring into the ocean.

"Hi," I said. "Water is cold... I predict a battle getting them into it this morning." Then I added hesitantly, "Are we still on for exploring this Saturday?"

Diego just stared at me for a moment and then said, "Are you still up for it?"

"Sure. I'm curious what we'll find going in that direction."

"OK," he said. "We'll head out after breakfast that day, unless your dad has a problem with that."

So, Dad had said something to him after all. I was curious for sure but did not want to show any hesitation. "Don't know why he should," I responded. "I'll see you then."

By this time, the boys were lumbering down the incline, not looking at all excited about today's lesson. Just to show them the water was fine today, I jumped in and got myself wet all over. "It's great," I said, trying not to shiver outwardly. "Come and jump in!"

One of the three boys was Jake, the smaller one who often helped in the fishing shack when we needed it. We bonded quite well, and he seemed to trust my instruction in the water. He seemed more unsure of himself than the other boys. After working on techniques for an hour, it had warmed up quite a bit, so I let the boys practice their skills in the water for a while longer even though they mostly just splashed each other and fooled around. When the session was over, we all went back to the dorm.

On Saturday morning, I packed some warmer clothes and snacks in my backpack and walked toward the southern trail shortly after breakfast. Diego was not at breakfast, so I wasn't even sure he would be coming along. Still, I was determined to go with or without him. I decided to take my phone because I knew the walk would be longer than any I had taken here before. However, with just one bar on my phone, I was skeptical of its use.

I proceeded down the trail for a while, not knowing when—or if—I would run into Diego. After a while, I decided to slow down a bit just in case he had a later start. I could tell right away that this was going to be a longer hike because, from where I was, I could not see or hear the ocean anymore. I came to a point in the trail where the path forked, and I just stood there for a while, trying to decide which path to take. Suddenly, I looked to my left and there was Diego, sitting on a rock not far down that path.

"I figured I would wait for you here," he said.

"Thanks," I said. "I wasn't sure you were coming today."

We walked down one of the paths for a while, not bothering to talk and instead just enjoying the weather and solitude surrounding us. It was a beautiful day, with birds singing and bees buzzing all around. After walking for about an hour, we came upon a little pond surrounded by rocks. We decided to take off our shoes and cool our feet in it.

I was dying to bring up my dad and ask Diego what, if anything, he had said to him. But I did not know how to start. After a few minutes, I said, "Do you have any sessions alone with my dad, or do you just work with the other counselors?"

He looked at me, smiled, and said, "Why? Are you curious what we talk about?"

"No," I said a little too quickly. "I was just wondering."

"I see your dad in a group session twice a week. Other than that, I mostly meet with the other counselors... though your dad did seek me out a couple of days ago to talk to me personally."

"Really? What about?" I asked as nonchalantly as I could.

"He wanted to ask me how I was doing and whether I was starting to fit into the routine. I had the feeling he was searching for ways to bring something else up but couldn't find the words."

"That's odd for my dad," I said. "Words are what he is best at."

"He did say that he noticed I was going off a lot on my own and questioned me about that."

"What did you say?" I asked casually.

"I told him I liked to be on my own sometimes, and we left it at that. I do know what he was trying to ask, Julia. He is not an idiot, and it's his job to be observant. But, unless he asks me directly about you, I'm not going to offer anything. Did he talk to you also?"

"Yes, at lunch that day we came back from the colony. He hinted that if we continued to hang out, it may hurt your relationships with the other guys. I don't really understand how that could happen, but I did decide to get more involved in activities with them so Dad could see that I'm friends with the other guys also and not just you."

"You don't think he's just afraid I'm a bad influence on you?" Diego asked with a grin.

"No, Dad's not like that. It sounded like he is more worried about you than me. Maybe he thinks I'm going to corrupt you," I retorted.

After a while, we started walking again, comfortably, with little talking involved. We stopped one more time for a quick snack, and I noticed it was starting to get cooler, so I put on my sweatshirt.

"I wonder what time it is. It's starting to get a lot darker over there," I said as I pointed out toward the direction in which we were walking. Our surroundings were changing. There were small trees here, and the path kept disappearing into tree groves and underbrush while taking different bends this way and that.

"Yeah, we should probably be heading back," said Diego, "but I was hoping we could reach the southern point before we do. I don't think it's much farther. If you listen carefully, you can hear the ocean now," he added.

We walked a bit further until we came to a cliff looking down a steep path to the ocean. We debated walking down the path but decided we should head back when, suddenly, we heard screaming coming from down below. We ran down the path and noticed an old fishing shack halfway down. We stopped to see if that was where the screaming was coming from, and again we heard it—this time, it was clearly coming from the water below.

Chapter 7

At the bottom of the path, we saw two figures floating in the water and desperately trying to hold on to an overturned boat. The waves were pushing them further out to sea. One smaller figure kept sinking under the water, and the bigger person was trying to hold him up and stay afloat as well.

Diego and I removed our shoes and sweatshirts and jumped in to try and help. As we got closer, I was shocked to see that the figures were Franklin and Jake! Diego and I immediately went to Jake and held on to him. We asked Franklin if he could swim to shore. He nodded his head and then swam back. Diego and I took turns swimming with Jake back to shore. It became easier as he was nodding in and out of consciousness and stopped fighting us as we swam.

Back on the shore, Franklin was laying on the beach and shivering, but he came to help us pull Jake out of the water and carry him to the beach. Remembering what I had learned from my classes, I started CPR on him, and Diego joined in to help. We stopped when Jake started coughing and pushed us away. We then remembered the small fishing shack up the path, so we decided to carry Jake there to try and warm him up. The weather was worsening, and it appeared that a storm was approaching. As Franklin and Diego carried Jake up the path, I checked my phone for service—nothing.

"Do you have a phone on you, Diego?"

"No," he answered while struggling to keep Jake upright. "We're not allowed to have our phones with us outside of our rooms."

The shack was not locked, so we rushed in. It consisted of just one open room with cupboards, a single cot, and a few boxes on the floor. There was also a small woodstove in the corner with some wood piled up next to it. Jake was now more alert but shivering like crazy. I ran out to look for some loose sticks and brush to put in the stove while Franklin and Diego got Jake out of his wet clothes. When I returned, he was wrapped in a blanket while sitting in a chair, and the guys were looking for matches. I noticed Franklin had stripped down also. He was now wearing Diego's sweatshirt with another blanket wrapped around his waist.

He noticed me looking and said with a smirk, "Like what you see?"

Ignoring him, I went to help Diego look for matches, which we finally found in one of the cupboards above a rough sink in the corner. Diego got the stove going, and the small room began to warm up. I took my discarded sweatshirt and my backpack and went out to the back of the shack. While there, I relieved myself quickly, put on my sweatshirt, and went back inside. By the time I returned, Jake looked a lot better and the guys were going through the few cupboards. They were looking for drinks and food.

"What in the world were you guys doing out in the water?" I finally asked Franklin.

Looking embarrassed, Jake answered instead by saying, "Diego mentioned where he was going, so we decided to follow in that direction. We were just exploring around when we found that old rowboat on the shore and decided to take it for a ride. We didn't get too far before it started filling up with water."

"And where were you expecting to go?" Diego asked sarcastically.

"Just exploring around," Franklin joined in. "Quit picking on him and let's find something to eat. I'm starving!" He continued searching like this was no big thing.

"This is serious, Franklin," I said. "Jake could have died out there if we did not come along, and maybe you also. We need to get back before it gets too dark or everyone will be out looking for us."

"It's already too dark, Julia," Diego said, looking at me seriously. "And it's starting to rain. It's at least a two-hour walk back to the compound. We don't even have a flashlight."

"I can use the light on my phone, but I'm not sure that's enough light to find our way back," I said hesitantly. Looking at Jake in the moment, he did not look like he could walk even a few feet, never mind a few miles.

"We'll have to stay here until early morning, and then we can set out," Diego said slowly. "I found some crackers in a tin, and the water in this sink doesn't smell too bad."

"I have another water bottle in my pack," I added. "Plus, here's another bar we can split up."

Diego went out to gather more sticks for the fire while I divvied up the food; it was not much, but it would have to do. Diego came back with the fuel supplies, and after adding them to the stove, he ate up his portion of the food. Jake lay down closest to the stove, and Franklin took his blanket and settled in one of the far corners. That left one thin sheet on the cot and a grubby looking pillow. Diego insisted that I take the cot, and he settled on the floor not far from the stove.

Discarding the pillow on the floor, I lay down and tried to get comfortable. I was worried sick about what would happen when we got back and wished I had mentioned to Dad where I was heading. I could not imagine what he thought when none of us showed up for dinner, and I was sure that there was a search party out there looking for us by now. *This is not going to end well,* I thought as I nodded off to sleep.

I woke up a few hours later, shivering and confused as to where I was. I sat up frightened when I heard something or someone stirring near me. "It's just me, Julia," Diego whispered. "I figured you may be getting cold, so I brought this to cover you." Diego slipped his flannel shirt over me, and I settled back in the bed, already somehow warmer.

"What about you? You must be freezing," I said quietly.

"I'm fine," he answered. "I just put some more wood on the fire. Try to get a little more sleep. The storm is passing quickly. We'll have to be leaving soon."

"I'm worried about my dad. He must be frantic worrying about me… about all of us. The whole crew must have been out all night looking for us."

"I went out a few times to see if I could hear them or see them," Diego responded. "I didn't hear anything. We'll head back in a couple of hours when I can make out the path." I lay back down, warmer than before, and tried to sleep again. As I dozed off, I wondered again how this efficient, mature boy could have ended up out here as a delinquent.

"Wake up, Julia," Diego said as he shook the bed a little. "It's light enough now that we can start walking back."

I looked around and noticed the other boys were still sleeping. Diego went over to wake them up as I slipped out the door to the back to go to the bathroom. When I got back, the guys were up and ready to go, though Jake looked for a minute like we were going to have to carry him again. I returned Diego's shirt to him, and we cleaned up the cabin the best we could. We headed out just as the sun was starting to come up. It was a nice, clear day as we started up the path back to the compound. I was nervous about what would happen when we got back. I'm sure my dad was a wreck, and we were all in a ton of trouble; I just was not sure how much.

The walk back was rough in the twilight, and we got lost a few times, but Diego, using my compass, was able to get us going in the right direction. We were hungry and cold, as our clothes from the adventure the day before had not completely dried. After an hour or so of walking, the sun came up enough to warm us, and I was just beginning to feel a lot better when I suddenly heard shouting coming from the approaching path. I was excited and apprehensive as we picked up our pace toward the shouting.

When I saw my dad and looked at his face, I started to tear up. Dan ran ahead of the group and shoved Diego out of the way to get to me. Dad caught up and calmed him down. He then told him to bring the boys back to his office immediately.

I ran to Dad, and he hugged me and asked if I was all right. I said I was and started to explain the situation, but he just held up his hand and said, "Not now. Let's just get you back to the compound." I could tell by his voice that I could not reason with him in that moment, and by the look he threw toward the boys, he was not listening to them either. We were all given water to drink before we continued our hike back to the compound.

On the way back, Dan and the other counselors walked ahead of us with the boys. There was little talking, though Jake tried to say a few things. He was immediately told to proceed without any talking also. When we finally returned to the compound, the boys were told to go immediately to the conference room. Dad told me to go back to the dorm to shower and rest.

"Ann will be over to check you out shortly," he said.

"But Dad, you need to let me explain first. And Ann needs to check out Jake; he's the one who had a problem," I protested.

He simply turned around and started walking toward his office saying, "We'll talk later after you're cleaned up. I'll send someone for you."

I felt like a little kid while heading back to my dorm, and I was frustrated that I could not explain myself before he started in on the guys. I was afraid Diego would be caught up in the whole boat story and, knowing him, he would not explain his huge part in the rescue.

I sat on my lower bunk, fuming at my dad for not letting me talk to him. A few minutes after I was there, I heard a knock on my door.

"OK if I come in, Julia?" Ann asked softly.

"Sure, come in," I answered. "I'm not sure why you're here, Ann. You should be checking out Jake. He had a boating accident and almost drowned. Diego and I had to use CPR to revive him, and then we had to warm him up."

"I'll check him out as soon as your dad is done talking to him, Julia. Can I just check you out and make sure you are fine? Were you out all night against your will? You can talk to me, and I'll keep anything you say private if you'd like."

"No," I answered, "I was not out against my will. Like I said, we had to help Jake warm up, and by the time we did it was too dark and stormy to head back. Luckily, we found an old shack that we stayed in until it was light enough to head back. My phone could not work out there, so I couldn't call anyone."

Ann just listened as she checked me out, and she left only after she was satisfied that I was fine. Hopefully, she would pass on to Dad what I had just told her and check to see that the boys were fine also.

Chapter 8

After Ann left, I showered, changed, and then sat on my bunk, just waiting to be "summoned." I must have dozed off, because about an hour later Maria was at my door to check up on me.

"You okay, Hun?" she asked. "Your dad wanted me to see how you are doing."

"I'm fine. Thanks. Can I go see him now?"

"He's still behind closed doors with the boys, and he just popped out for a second to have me check on you. How about coming over for some lunch? Or, if you prefer, I could bring it to you."

"Have the boys had lunch yet?" I asked her. It irritated me that I was being treated with kid gloves while the boys were being interrogated next door before even being fed.

"Not yet," Maria answered, "but if you come over now then maybe you can help me put together something for them."

I knew she was just saying that to get me up and going, but it seemed like a better alternative than just staying in my room and waiting to talk to Dad. I got up and followed her to the cafeteria. When I entered the hall, the smell of soup overwhelmed me, and I realized I was starving. I followed Maria into the kitchen, and we began making sandwiches.

I kept looking at the door to the cafeteria, hoping to see the boys and Dad enter the room, when Maria finally said to me, "You want to talk about it?"

"I don't understand why Dad won't let me explain and tell my side of the story," I said.

"He will eventually, Hun. Right now, he's too upset to deal with you. That's my guess. He'll get to you when he calms down. Remember, he's also responsible for all those boys. He took them under his wing when he started this project. It hit him hard when none of you showed up last night. I'm willing to bet he had more faith that you were all right than those boys. They haven't always made the best of decisions, I'm guessing. He and his team have been working hard to get them on the right path."

"So, he blames me for all of this, I suppose?" I asked moodily, wondering if I did blame myself for part of it also.

"Of course not. He'll get to you soon, I'm sure," Maria concluded with a hug and wink. "Meanwhile, let's get these sandwiches and cookies out on a tray for everyone. Then I can knock on the door and see if I can motivate them to come to lunch."

When the boys finally came to the cafeteria, Maria and I got busy serving the food to everyone. The boys sat together at one table and avoided me completely. When I finally sat down by myself to eat, Dad approached the table and asked me to join him in his office.

"Bring along your lunch," he said, "and we'll eat together in there."

I followed him hesitantly, not knowing what kind of reaction or reprimand to expect from him.

After we were settled at his conference table, I said flippantly, "Now am I finally going to get the chance to give you my side of the story?"

"The boys all agreed that this was completely their fault and you had nothing to do with their decision to take the boat. I assume that is correct. I'm simply confused what you were doing there to discover them and help them right at that time when they were in trouble?" Dad responded.

I thought for a minute and then said, "The boys? Diego had nothing at all to do with taking that boat."

"Well, according to their story," he elaborated, "they were exploring and came upon the boat and decided to take it out for a ride. That's when it overturned, and you came along to save the day. Apparently, it was too late then to make it back, so you all decided to stay the night in some shed that you found."

"Diego had nothing to do with taking that boat, Dad. He and I were just out for a hike when we heard yelling. We ran down the path and saw them struggling in the water. Both Diego and I helped save the boys, though it was a close call for Jake at first. Luckily, Diego and I knew CPR and helped revive him."

"Well then, that means he made up a story on top of everything else. This program only works if based on truth, and that doesn't seem to be happening here. Julia, if you had only told me your plans rather than sneaking off, I would have known where you were heading. I suggested that you not spend so much time with Diego and you went behind my back anyway. Diego is obviously trying to protect you by not getting you involved in this. But in the process, he lied to me, which is even worse."

"I don't know why he said that Dad, but maybe he was also trying to protect the boys and help back up their story. I don't know what I would have done if he wasn't there. He was so calm and took charge of getting the boys to safety and to the shack for warmth. He shouldn't be punished at all."

"That's not up to you, Julia. There will have to be some repercussions over this incident for the boys. As for you, you are to stay away from the boys except for activities that you are involved in, and there will be no more hanging out with Diego for the rest of this summer."

"Oh great, Dad, so now I'm a prisoner here also. That's not fair and you know it. We were just walking and talking. I finally have a friend here who I can talk to, and you act like he's a hardened criminal. I thought that type of thinking was against your policies here. But, I guess, they go out the window when dealing with your precious daughter."

I stormed out the door after not even touching my lunch. Dad called my name as I left, but I just ignored him. I was determined to call Mom and see what she could do about getting me off this stupid island as soon as possible.

Unfortunately, when I finally reached Mom, she did not have any sympathy for me at all. Apparently, Dad had talked to her last night, several times, and she had been a wreck before I was found. Now, they were on the same page that I should stay and "learn my lesson." *Great*, I thought, *they pick this time to finally agree and begin working together.*

Feeling that I had no one to turn to, I decided to work on my paper and delve into the depressing loneliness of staying on a deserted island—well, at least now it felt deserted—in the middle of nowhere by myself. I was liking where my paper was going when someone knocked on my door.

"Thought you would be hungry again," Maria said. "Here are some brownies right out of the oven. And some milk to wash them down with, too."

"Thanks, Maria," I said gloomily. "I won't be over to help you with dinner tonight if that's all right with you. I'm quite tired again, and I think I'll just work on my paper some more and then go right to bed."

Chapter 9

I avoided talking to Dad for the next couple of days. Maria and I had previously planted a small vegetable and flower garden behind the main building, and I had noticed it needed weeding the last time I was there. So, on the second day after the incident, I decided to skip breakfast and instead work there in solitude. I was not working too long when I saw someone come around the building toward me.

It was Jake, looking a bit guilty and hesitant. "Sorry about all this, Julia. Franklin talked me into exploring with him, and I was happy to get away for a while. We got lost but then reached the ocean and found the boat, and, well, you know the story from there."

"I'm just not sure how Diego got caught up in your story, Jake?" I asked.

"He just joined in as if he were there with us all along. I think he was trying to protect you and didn't want to admit he was with you. He gave us a look, and we just went along with his story," Jake added sheepishly. "We've lost all free-time privileges for a while, plus no phones or computers until further notice."

"Same with Diego?" I asked.

"Yeah. He's standing by his story that he was with us the whole time. Not sure why he said that. It didn't make much difference with our punishment, and it definitely hurt him... especially since he can't see you," Jake answered.

"Why do you say that? Did he say something to you?" I asked.

"No, but he's been moping around and looking like he's lost his best friend. I'm sorry, Julia, that I got you guys involved. Franklin doesn't say it, but I know he feels bad also."

I spent the rest of the day in my room, trying to decide what to do about the situation. I worked on my paper a little more and wrote a few meaningless emails to my friends, hoping they would send back some gossip that would distract me from the doldrums. After helping at dinner that night, I went to bed early and tossed and turned all night.

I hung around aimlessly for the rest of the next day, feeling sorry for myself. I avoided running into anyone, and I mostly just stayed in my room again working on my paper and emailing my friends. I was glad I hadn't shared with Meg my feelings for Diego because I'm sure I would be getting another lecture from her by now. I snuck into the kitchen at one point in the day and made some sandwiches to eat in my room. I then just continued to work on my research some more. I was really starting to get into it, too, and the more I learned about this island the more fascinated I became. Before I knew it, it was midnight, and I realized that no one had come to check on me all day. I guess they got the message that I needed time to myself.

I woke up late the next day around lunchtime, and I ate in the kitchen with Maria. I then decided to walk down by the water and do some thinking. The more I thought about things that had happened, the more upset I got—but I was not sure with whom I was most upset. Dad never gave me the chance to explain myself first, which would have made the story clear to him before he talked to the boys. Diego never should have lied to my dad about being with the boys either. I still was not sure why he did that.

And then I got to myself. It is true that if I had told Dad where I was going—and with whom I was going—the fallout would have been much less severe. I could have been brave and

45

convinced him that we were just friends and that I simply enjoyed Diego's company. Dad was a decent person, and I probably could have reasoned with him. At least then, he would have had an idea where we were that night and where to search for us. I was so consumed by my thoughts that I did not hear anyone approaching from behind me.

"What are you doing here alone in such deep thought?" Dan said while approaching me. For some reason, I was uncomfortable to be caught here alone with him.

"Just resting and enjoying the scenery," I quickly lied. "What's up?"

"I missed you when you didn't show up at archery class this morning and wondered where you were," he said before sitting down next to me.

I felt a bit uncomfortable with how close he got to me, so I jumped up and started collecting my things. "I was just going to head back," I answered. "Did the class go well?"

"Yes, but Diego didn't show up also, so I wanted to make sure he wasn't here with you."

"He wasn't," I answered abruptly. "And even if he were, I don't know what business it would be to you."

I turned to walk away, and he grabbed my hand tightly. "He's bad news, Julia. I want you to stay far away from him."

"I don't think that's any business of yours, Dan," I said, yanking my hand away from him. I then walked quickly up the path to the compound, feeling more nervous than I ever had since arriving on the island. I made a mental note not to be alone with Dan if I could help it. I wanted to tell Dad about the interaction, but since we were not even talking at this time, I went back to my room feeling more alone than ever.

I spent the rest of that day doing some more research and writing down notes in my journal. I did go the cafeteria for dinner and to help Maria. I ate in the kitchen with her, and she let me brood without asking any questions.

The next day, I was scheduled to be in the fishing shack to help with a craft class. I wanted to skip it, but since the project was my idea, I felt I had to be there. I held back going early so I would not get there before the boys. But when I did get there, no one was around. I was just about the head out, thinking that the class must have been canceled, when Dan walked in and shut the door.

"I take it you didn't check the board today, Julia," he said. "This class was canceled today."

"Why?" I asked. "I thought all these group activities were the basis Dad's program."

"I'm changing the program around, Julia. I've decided to limit who can participate in my activities," Dan answered as he walked toward me.

"Does Dad know about this?" I asked as I sidestepped around him and headed toward the door. Just as I was turning the handle to leave, Dan grabbed me from behind and started to hug me.

"Stop it!" I screamed and tried to push him away.

"You need to calm down, Julia," he said and continued to hold me tightly.

"Let me go!" I screamed again and tried to wiggle free of his grip.

Just then the door opened, and Diego rushed in. "What's going on here?" he asked, approaching Dan after he saw my frightened face.

"Get out of here!" Dan yelled. "Class has been canceled, and you don't belong here." By this time, Dan had released me but was still too close for me to run.

"I'll leave, but Julia's coming with me," Diego said, walking casually toward us.

"You come any closer and I'll tell her father what you guys were up to in here," Dan threatened.

"Go ahead then," Diego said and reached out for my hand, which I took quickly and headed for the door.

We ran together back to the main building, and when I turned to thank Diego, he was already gone. I headed right to Dad's office, but he was in there with a few other counselors talking. I decided to walk in anyway, and by the look on my face he knew right away that it was serious. He dismissed the others and told me to sit down.

I proceeded to tell him everything that had happened, starting with the incident down at the beach the day before. I could see he had to restrain himself to keep a controlled face when I got to the part where Dan tried to hug me and would not let me go. When I was done talking, he stood up and held out his arms. I fell into them and started crying, releasing all the tension that had built up over the last few days.

When I calmed down a bit, I turned to him and said, "I don't know what would have happened if Diego didn't show up, Dad."

Dad just hugged me for a long time and then insisted that I go see Ann for a checkup and talk, even though I told him I was fine. Ann was sympathetic and understanding, and she did not press me to talk more than I wanted to. It was nice to talk to her, and she did remind me a lot of my mom, whom I was missing a lot.

Chapter 10

Things changed quickly after that day. The next morning, I was hesitant to go to the shed in case I ran into Dan, so I wandered out front to get some air. Glancing out to the ocean, I noticed the ferry coming our way. It was not the typical supply day, so I was surprised to see it approaching. Then I saw the motorized cart come around the corner with bags packed on it, and in the cart were Dad and Dan. Not wanting them to see me, I quickly slipped back into the building and went to talk to Maria to see if she knew what was happening.

"He just didn't work out with your dad's program is what I heard, Julia," she said. "He's leaving the island today to go back to the mainland."

I had mixed feeling since I knew he was a crucial part of Dad's limited staff, but I also had an overwhelming feeling of relief. Fishing for more information and wondering how much Maria really knew, I asked, "Who's going to take over all his sessions and work with the outdoor activities?"

"Not sure, Hun," Maria answered, "but your dad will work it out. He's got some good volunteer interns here with him; perhaps one or two of them can step up and take over with the activities at least. And I'm sure you'll be a big help when needed."

Not sure what to do next, I decided to go back to my room and write to Meg about the latest happenings. But when I tried to put in all in writing, it all seemed too personal to share. Also, not knowing exactly what the outcome really was with Dan, I decided to wait until another time to fill her in.

I then wondered about calling Mom, but I had a feeling that Dad had done that already, so I decided to wait until after I talked to him today. I hadn't worked on my paper for a while, so I opened it up on my computer and started to reread it. After doing so, it occurred to me that the most interesting part was the reference to the leper colony that was here years ago. I decided to do some more research on that era and was overwhelmed with what I found.

It is amazing how looking at life from another perspective can put your problems in a different light. What these people had to endure here and how much they had to give up really opened my eyes to how little my problems were. Most of all, though, I started to see the similarities between what the dedicated doctors and staff in the leper colony did in comparison with my dad and his staff here. They, like the staff from years ago, had to move here to help these boys and sacrificed their personal lives, if only for just one summer. Maybe that would be the direction my paper would go in—how dedication and having a goal can help others and perhaps change lives. I was excited as I started on my new direction.

In fact, I became so involved with my writing that it was a moment before I heard the knocking at my bedroom door. I got up to answer it, and Dad was standing there.

"Hi, Hun, can we talk?"

"Sure, do you want to come in or should I meet you at your office?" I asked him.

"Here's fine," he said as he came in and took a seat on my bottom bunk, facing my desk.

"What are you working on there?" he asked.

"A new direction on my essay for school. I'll tell you more about it when it's more developed."

"Well," he said, "there's going to be a few changes around here, and I wanted to fill you in on them."

Dad went on to tell me that Dan had resigned his post and was heading back to the mainland. He said he gave him a choice of doing that or being brought up on charges of assault on a minor. I did not say anything, but I watched his face for some signs of remorse and saw none. He continued to say that all of Dan's sessions and responsibilities would be divided up among the other counselors, which they accepted with no problem. His duties in the fishing shack and with outdoor activities would be taken over by Mike, an intern that had been showing promise. Mike was to become part of the regular staff moving forward.

He hesitated there and added, "He will need a lot of help, though. Are you still up for volunteering with that project?"

"Of course," I said quickly, "whatever I can do to help."

"Also," he went on, "I am assigning Diego to help out with all the outdoor activities as well. He will get credit as a student helper and will report to Mike, the new junior counselor."

By the look of surprise on my face, he added quickly, "Yes, I have changed my mind about him and you. I talked to your mom for a while today, and she helped me put things in a better perspective. She said I should have trusted you more, and I agree. I think I may have over-reacted and did not give him or you the benefit of the doubt. However, from now on, I expect complete honesty from the two of you. And I am going to start planning more social outings for everyone—group outings—so you and the counselors can get to know all the boys in a more personal way. I need your help with this plan if you're willing."

"Wow, Dad, for sure," I answered quickly. "When does all this start?"

"The new activity center will open in a few days. Mike is already over in the shed, looking over things there. Do you want to go and help him get oriented?"

"Does he know that Diego and I will be helping him?"

"Yes, and he was excited to have the extra help. So, what do you say, are you back on the team?" he asked as he was getting up.

"For sure," I said, excited to get back into a routine where I could help. The fact that Diego would be helping also was just an added benefit.

We headed to the cafeteria together for lunch. Dad had Mike sit with us so I could get to know him better. He was younger than the other counselors but seemed quiet and respectful in front of Dad. He said he did have some sailing experience, which was good because that was my weakest area. He was excited and eager to get going and asked me if I was available after lunch to help him with a project he had in mind. I told him I would be over right after I helped Maria clean up in the kitchen.

When I got to the building, I immediately noticed a change. Mike had opened all the shutters over the windows and propped open the door of the shack. I had never realized how musty it had become in there with everything so closed up before. He also was in the process of opening two quarts of blue paint. There were tarps spread over all the shelves, cabinets, and tables.

"I guess we're painting today?" I asked with a smile.

"Yes, if you're up for it," he answered. "I felt this space needed a pick-me-up, and your dad said I could use any of the paint in the storage room, so I picked this color. What do you think?"

"It's great," I said encouragingly, "Where to you want me to start?"

"How about you start with the cabinets, Julia. I thought maybe those could be painted white," he said.

"Good plan," I said while reaching for a smock that would cover most of my clothes.

We had been working for about an hour when Diego walked in and introduced himself to Mike. He just gave me a quick grin and proceeded to roll up his sleeves and grab a paintbrush. The sun was shining in all the windows, and already the shed was looking like a brand-new space.

I had been here on the island for about one month now, and I had another month to go. I was finally excited about the new social plans and being able to pursue my friendship with Diego without sneaking around. Little did I know, however, just how much things would change after that day.

Chapter 11

Dad called me into his office a couple of days later, and I was surprised to see Diego in there as well. Diego was looking over a map that was spread over Dad's conference table. He smiled when I walked in, so it did not appear to be a new crisis that was brewing.

"It dawned on me, Julia," Dad started in without looking up from the map, "that you and the boys stayed over in a shed on the south side of the island. Well, this was always a private island, only used for research and humanitarian purposes, so I couldn't imagine why there would be a shed there... and the boys said it looked like it was in use recently?"

"Yes, Dad. We found food in the cupboards and wood that had been collected for a fire near the stove."

"I'm having Diego show me on this rough map whereabouts you found the shack. I think we should go back and check it out. If there's anything suspicious there, I should be calling the police on the mainland, or even the Coast Guard, to come check it out. You two want to join me on a little hike early tomorrow morning?"

The next morning, we left shortly after breakfast. This time, I was careful to bring extra food and water just in case. The walk seemed to go a little faster since we knew where we were going, and Diego's natural sense of direction had us approaching the cliff in just under two hours. We walked down the path to the shed and approached it warily. We decided to knock on the door before entering, not sure what to expect.

The door was unlocked, just like it had been the previous time. When no one answered, we decided to go in. We looked around the shed and noticed not much had changed since

54

the last time we had been there—but there was a backpack sitting on the bed, which was not there before. I pointed it out and said, "That is new here. Someone has been here since we left."

Diego picked it up and looked inside before throwing it back on the cot quickly. "That looks like heroin. We should get out of here—fast!"

"Whoever left it there can't be far away," Dad said. "Let's get back to the compound so I can call the authorities. I wonder how they are getting here. I'm sure they're not using our dock."

"We could sneak down to the beach and see what they're using for a watercraft," Diego said, getting into the excitement of it all.

I, on the other hand, was not in the mood to run into whoever was here on this side of the island, and I suggested that we head back and get help. Fortunately, Dad agreed with me, and we retreated up the path toward the camp. As we were leaving, however, we heard talking coming up the path from the beach.

"Quick! Hide over here," Diego said as he pulled me toward the woods surrounding the shed. Dad quickly followed and we all lay down just as two men were approaching the shed.

"Are you sure you put the backpack on the bed just as we found it, Diego?" Dad whispered.

"Yes… I'm quite sure," Diego answered. "If they come running out, though, stay hidden here, as I'm not sure we can outrun them, especially if they have guns."

Everything happened so fast after that. One of the men ran out and started looking around. Before I knew what was happening, Diego stood up, walked toward the man, and blurted out, "Hey, man, I got lost and was hoping I could find some water in your shed."

I wanted to run toward him also, but Dad held his hand over my mouth and gestured for me to stay low. The man dragged Diego into the shed and Dad grabbed me. We then started running up the path toward the direction of the compound. After a few minutes, I pulled my hand away and said, "Dad, we can't just leave him there. We have to go back!"

"No, Julia. We're going for help," he whispered. "It won't be any good if they catch all of us, and then no one will be able to get help for Diego."

I was a wreck, but I ran with Dad and made it back to the compound in record time. Dad quickly ran into his office and contacted the local police from the mainland. After talking to them for what seemed like an eternity, they agreed to contact the Coast Guard as well as the police boat on Cuttyhunk, the nearest island.

It seemed like forever until the police boat arrived, and after chatting for a few minutes, we jumped on and took off. The police had been in contact with the Coast Guard and directed them to meet us on the south side of the island with Dad's directions. When we got to the other side, the water was too rough for the boat to dock close to shore. I wanted the police to jump in and go save Diego, but they said they had to wait for the Coast Guard. We also noticed a larger vessel anchored closer to the shore, but there was no movement on it that we could detect with the binoculars the police offered us.

When the Coast Guard ship arrived, it tied up next to the police boat, and two of the policemen jumped onboard. They then lowered a motorized vessel off the ship, and a few authorities rode toward the shore. I wanted to go, too, but was told that I would just be in the way. Dad, who looked as nervous as I was, just held me but did not try to talk. He knew better.

It seemed like forever before we saw figures coming back toward the beach. Using the binoculars, all I saw at first were the authorities and two men, who were handcuffed, walking in front of them. My heart was beating so fast—where was Diego!

Then I saw him. Diego was behind them, walking toward the beach with the other officer helping him. He looked a bit beat up, but I did notice he was mostly walking on his own. What a relief.

When they got back to the boat, the Coast Guard officials helped the two officers and Diego on to the police boat, and they took the two other men aboard their ship. I ran to Diego and tried to hug him, but the police held me back. "He's a bit banged up," the officer said. "We're going to check him out before anyone touches him or talks to him."

"What do you mean 'talks to him?'" Dad asked. "He didn't do anything. He just stepped up when we were almost discovered, like I told you, and diverted the men from finding us."

"We understand that," said the officer, "but we need to bring him back to Cuttyhunk, get him checked out, and then interrogate him on what he knows about the two men."

"He doesn't know anything more than we do," Dad said emphatically. "So, we're going also. And he will not be talking to you at all until I can arrange a lawyer to be with him."

"No, that won't be necessary, I'm sure," said the second officer. "Of course, you can come along. We just need to get his statement about what happened after he entered the shed with the men."

On the way to Cuttyhunk, Dad called the camp to let the counselors know he would not be back for a while. The officers finally let me sit next to Diego if one of them was near us the whole time. Diego had a bloodied eye and a bruised cheek, but he seemed to be moving well enough. He said he was fine and whispered to me that he had convinced the men that he was by himself—after first taking a few punches—and told them he was just exploring the shed for water. He was not sure what their plans were for him, and he was just plotting a way to escape in his head before the officers arrived.

When we got to Cuttyhunk, the officers took us to the local health clinic to have Diego checked out. After an "all clear" from the doctor, they drove us to their station, where they told Diego to write down everything that happened. Since Dad and I had been in the shed also, they took us to another room and had us write our version of what happened as well. When they were satisfied that our stories matched, they said we could go, but they told us not to leave the island.

"I'm in charge of the program on Penikese, so I'm going back there. And Julia and Diego are going with me," Dad said emphatically. "If not, then I guess we do need that lawyer I asked for originally."

"As long as you stay on that island until you hear from us, then that is fine," the second officer said. "When the Coast Guard finishes their investigation, we'll let you know. They may need Diego back to testify against the men."

"And we'll be needing a ride back to Penikese," Dad said with authority.

Chapter 12

When we got back to Penikese, everyone met us at the dock, boys and counselors included. Diego went to get checked out by Ann while Dad and I filled in everyone with the details of the long day.

We all met again in the cafeteria for a late dinner that Maria had warmed up for us. Though the boys and the staff had already eaten that evening, they stayed close and enjoyed the extra dessert that Maria had put out for everyone. Looking around the cafeteria, I noticed a big difference in the atmosphere. The boys and the staff were sitting together on various tables, all comparing notes on what had happened and surmising about what would happen to the criminals.

Diego and I sat together holding hands under the table. I was not very hungry, but I tried to eat what Maria had dished out for me. Dad kept telling everyone that Diego was a hero and that if he hadn't done what he did, he was not sure what the outcome would have been.

The next morning, I woke up to heavy rain and fog. I checked the bulletin board on my way into breakfast to see if the day's activities were going on as scheduled, and I was pleased to see that they were. After breakfast, I headed to the craft building to see what Mike had planned for the rainy day. When I walked in, I was stunned by the shack's transformation. Even though it was a gloomy day, the bright-colored walls added life to the room. Also, Mike had music playing from a boom box he had set up in the corner. Several tables were also set up with supplies to make our rope bracelets.

"Wow," I said. "You got started early this morning."

"Yes", he answered. "When I saw the rain, I decided to come over here and see what projects we could do instead. I liked the idea you had written down about the rope bracelets, so I decided to go in that direction. I hope you have the time today to help me with my scheduled groups?"

"Sure," I said. "Do you need a tutorial before we get started?"

For the next hour, I showed him how to get started making the bracelets and how to adjust them for size. The boys trickled in throughout the morning in small groups, and they seemed surprised as well by the warmth of the room and the casualness of the atmosphere. By lunchtime, several of them had finished their bracelets or had asked to take them back to their room to work on them there.

Diego came in with the last group, looking a bit tired and with a huge shiner, but he had a big smile on his face when he saw the room. He just winked at me and set about making a bracelet for his stepmom. I had set up some buckets of water and dye in the corner of the room in case the boys wanted a different color for the bracelets after they were finished.

Diego came up to me to check on what colors I had available. He slipped his bracelet into the bucket with pink dye in it and asked, "How long should it stay in there?"

"It depends how pink you want it to be," I responded with a teasing grin. "Are you heading over to lunch now? We can check it after lunch if you want it dark pink."

We then walked together down the path to the cafeteria and sat down with some of the other guys who were already there. I felt strange sitting there at first, but Dad had said he wanted me to start fitting in with all the boys, so I stayed where I initially sat. They seemed to accept me after the initial awkwardness of the moment. They treated Diego like a hero, who kept answering questions about the day before. Of course, he downplayed his role in the events and tried to divert the conversation.

When I walked up to the counter to get my lunch, I passed Dad, who was at a table talking to some of the other workers. He winked at me and continued talking, so I smiled as I walked by.

The rest of the day passed quickly. Soon, everyone was finishing up their bracelets and cleaning up. The boys were excited when they came to collect their finished products, and many expressed their desire to work on some again in the future. Mike and I agreed that we would continue this project on the next indoor day.

At dinner that evening, Dad asked me if I could schedule a meeting with him the next day to go over some plans and ideas for the upcoming weeks at camp. I was excited to go back to my room and write down some ideas, which included:

- Plan some hiking trips, where the boys could explore the rest of the island.
- Since they enjoy the rope course so much, build an extended one down on the southern shore, where there are appropriate trees to work with.
- Have some music/game nights after dinner, where we could all relax together.
- Plan a weekly picnic at the beach.
- Have the boys work on some research with me on the leper colony that existed here. (Maybe we could even assign them a person's name to see what they could find out about them.)

I knew some of these ideas were ambitious, but I also knew that Dad had big plans for his school; if these could not all happen right away, perhaps they could be put in motion for next summer. I was shocked to suddenly find myself excited about the possibility of coming back again next year—maybe even as an intern since I am rather good at setting up this social stuff. *I guess I may be getting a little ahead of myself,* I thought as I turned off my light and fell into the best sleep I've had since coming to the island.

Chapter 13

Upon arriving at the beach the next morning, I was surprised to see Diego and the boys already there and set to get started. The ocean was starting to get a little warmer now, so there were fewer complaints, and I could see the boys making some progress and gaining confidence in the water.

After the session, the boys went to breakfast, and Diego and I stayed behind to collect the water supplies. On the way back up the trail, I almost slipped while carrying one of the bins, and Diego grabbed my hand and helped me up. We walked together the rest of the way, holding hands the entire time. I had never felt more comfortable with a friend in my life before that moment—especially a boy.

We dropped hands as we entered the cafeteria and sat down with Jake and Roberto. After a minute, I walked into the kitchen to check on Maria. I wanted to see if she needed any help since we were a little late for breakfast, but she was all set with two other boys already assisting her. I told her we were fine with cereal and muffins and that she did not have to make anything special for us. She thanked me.

After breakfast, the boys went off into their planned sessions with the counselors, and I walked over to the shed to see if Mike needed my help. He was setting up the small sailboats since it seemed like a perfect day for it. We carried the boats down to the shore and rigged them up. I agreed to take one of the boys out with me, and Mike would take the other, keeping his boat nearby in case I got in trouble. For these classes, we only had two boys at a time, so it was easier to handle.

The morning went by quickly, and because the weather was quite calm and smooth, I had no trouble managing the boat. My last student was Diego, so I relaxed even more knowing that he was a strong swimmer if things went awry. We sailed a little away from the other boat and simply enjoyed the slight wind and gorgeous day.

"Ready to take over?" I asked him.

"You think I'm ready?" he answered hesitantly.

"Sure," I said before handing him the rudder.

We had sailed out a little farther than I had planned at this point, so I suggested he tack and point us back to the shore. He did it perfectly, and I think I was prouder of him than he was of himself. It must have shown on my face, too, because after we came to shore and helped Mike carry the equipment back to the shed, Diego asked, "Why the face back on the boat? You didn't expect me to do as well as I did?"

"Not at all," I responded. "Just super proud of how you handled the boat and surprised how quickly you pick up new things."

He seemed pleased by my response as we headed back to the main building for lunch. We sat down with some other boys and ate in a comfortable silence, just enjoying hearing their chatter back and forth about their sailing experiences. After lunch, I went to my scheduled meeting with Dad.

He seemed really impressed with all my ideas, but he brought me back to reality when he reminded me that we now had a little less than a month left to go at camp. He put me in charge of setting up the weekly picnics, with Maria's help, and agreed that Diego and I could arrange the hikes since we had already voyaged around much of the island. He did say we would have to bring counselors along with us, but I agreed that the two extra interns would work out fine. He liked the idea of the music and game nights as well. I suggested that we get

Franklin to help with those, as it seemed he was always playing music or rapping to himself. Also, he had a real sense of what the others liked. He talked me into holding off on the rope course idea until next summer; that would give us more time to find the perfect spot for it and investigate who owned the little shack on that part of the island.

That just left my research idea. Though Dad did like it, he felt it would be too much to add into the schedule right now. However, he thought it would be a great thing to add next year, and he said he would try to purchase more computers by then to accommodate the activity. As I was getting up to leave, Dad told me he had some news—Diego would be heading back to the mainland the next day in order to make a statement to the Coast Guard about his interaction with the smugglers. I asked if I could go with him, but Dad said they only wanted Diego. Dad explained that he had to talk them into letting him be present also. They would be leaving first thing in the morning, and he was not sure when they would be back. He had hired a private boat to pick them up and drop them back off at the island.

I was worried the entire next day, and I kept going out and hanging around the dock, just waiting for their return. Several of the boys were also present there throughout the day, pretending to fish and trying not to look concerned—though I could tell they were worried also. Around 4:00 p.m., as I was just sitting and reading on the dock, Franklin came and sat down next to me.

"I'm sure they're OK, Julia," he said. "This is normal—getting all the witnesses involved to clarify what they know about the suspects."

It seemed so strange having Franklin trying to make me feel better. Usually, he never said more than a couple of words to me. "I'm just worried," I responded. "It seems like they've been gone so long. You don't think the officials are blaming Diego for something and are holding him there, do you?"

"No, I don't," he said quickly. "And besides, do you really think Dr. Cooper would let that happen? Since he's there with him, Julia, I wouldn't be worried at all."

I wanted to believe him, but then why were all these boys out here waiting for them also? Just as I was about to make that argument, I saw the boat approaching the pier. Dad and Diego jumped off carrying packages and looking pleased with themselves.

I ran to greet them, and Diego smiled and held up a bag saying, "We brought back McDonald's for everyone!"

Dad smiled and handed me another bag, and we started walking back to the cafeteria. "Everything went fine, Julia. Diego was very professional and answered all their questions. They already had a lot of other offenses on those two guys, so they appreciated Diego's cooperation."

"I was so worried, Dad," I responded. "I wished you had called me and let me know."

"Sorry, Julia, we were kind of enjoying ourselves and made an adventure out of the trip. After leaving the Coast Guard station, we walked along the pier and had a long talk about Diego's goals and future. Then we went out for lunch and ended up buying extra for everyone here. I'm sure Maria won't mind heating all this up for the crew and the boys."

We headed up to the cafeteria together, and I walked in to help Maria with the food. When I walked back out to help serve it, I noticed that someone had pushed together all the tables, and everyone was sitting together talking. I looked over at Dad—who was standing in the corner smiling—and realized that this scene was exactly what he had hoped for with this endeavor. I was so happy for him, and I was also so proud to be a part of it all.

Chapter 14

The next two weeks went by quickly, and I spent all my free time jotting down more and more ideas about how to improve and personalize the camp. I was beginning to understand Dad's excitement about building a program from the bottom up. I spent some time searching out areas for our music and game nights. I was a bit discouraged by the time I had finished looking around, though, as I had found no comfortable spaces for the boys and staff to hang out together in the evenings. I sought out Dad to share my dilemma, and I saw him just as he was walking into the cafeteria. I asked him if we could sit privately together.

Over breakfast, I shared my frustration, and he recognized there might be a problem. "All the rooms here were made for classrooms, small group sessions, or offices," he said. "I did hope to have money in my budget to set up a recreation hall of some type before the camp opened, but it was not in the cards for this year."

"So, it's something you are hoping to have for next year?" I asked, getting excited as I felt another idea brewing in my brain.

"Yes, hopefully, if I can raise some extra funds. I need to do a lot of traveling this winter to share my vision for this type of school, and hopefully in the process I'll gain some sponsors."

"Here's an idea, Dad… what if we had all the supplies for an extra building dropped off here before the camp started next year, and you could incorporate the building of the rec hall with the boys involved? That way they would be learning a skill and gaining confidence at the same time!"

"That would be a very big undertaking, Julia," he said less enthusiastically. "I would have to hire a project manager and get building permits, and who knows what else?"

"Yes, but think about how much would be gained in the process, Dad. The boys still seem to have a lot of down time, and I don't see them learning too many skills, other than things they probably won't apply when they get back to their own environments."

He seemed discouraged by my words, and I was just about to take them back when he said, "Let me think about it, Julia. It's not a bad concept, and it would really boost up my program here. But I see it possibly causing more headaches than it's worth."

I felt our talk was over and got up to leave. But before I did, I turned around and said, "Also, Dad, keep in mind that Diego is a very capable worker, and he hopes to be an engineer someday. He could be a big help with this one also."

He looked at me for a moment and then said, "You're assuming, Julia, that Diego will be back here next year. It's my goal that he will be out of the program by then and off to other things. He really wants to get a better-paying job, and he wants to start helping his family."

I thought about that for a second and asked, "What about if he came back as a junior counselor or an intern? Some of your interns here are pretty young, and he's turning eighteen pretty soon, I think."

He seemed to hesitate for a second before saying, "Julia, Diego probably didn't even belong here this summer. His offense was not really that bad, and I probably could have testified to get him off with a warning. I didn't want him to be home for the summer when his stepbrother just finished his time, so I talked the judge into assigning him here with me. I shouldn't be telling you any of this, kiddo, but I know you care about him and have been wondering about things. What you are suggesting would be fine in a perfect world, but I'm sure I wouldn't have the money to spare to pay him."

"Just a thought anyway, Dad," I said as I walked toward the door. When I got to the door, I turned around once more and added, "Thanks for sharing that, Dad. I know you care about him also, as you do all the boys. I'm hoping I can come back and be part of the program next year... and you won't have to pay me." He smiled and winked as I left.

The rest of that week went by quickly. Besides my swimming lessons, yoga classes, and helping Mike in the activity center, I had also made plans with Maria for our first seaside picnic, which was to be held on Saturday. We planned the food together. Mike, Diego, and I added some fun water activities for the event, too, if the weather permitted. We decided to stick with only bringing down the kayaks and canoes.

For the following Sunday, Diego and I planned a hike up to the leper colony site, which would also include a short informative speech. We would leave shortly after breakfast that day and be back by lunch so that the boys could have some free time for themselves. Since Sunday was supposed to be completely free for them, the hike would be on a sign-up-only basis, even though most of the guys we mentioned it to already seemed somewhat interested in going.

And as for the music and game nights, I met with Franklin a few times to gauge whether he would be interested in helping me plan them. At first, he did not seem too enthusiastic about hanging around with everyone after dinner, especially if some of the adults would be there also. But when I told him he would have full control over the music choices, he showed a bit of interest. I asked him to first help me find a space to use, as he seemed to like the idea of exploring as well. We decided on an unused larger classroom, where we could move the desks out of the way and bring in some larger office chairs and the small couch that we found in a storage room. He then set about planning the music, and I found some games, cards, and magazines from one of the larger session rooms. They did not look like they had been touched all summer, but they did help the room look a bit more casual and fun. What we really needed were some computers to use for video games, but that, I decided, would be something to think about for next summer. I could not believe how excited I was getting about the idea of spending another summer here—and this one was not even over yet.

The picnic on Saturday went over great. Everyone started heading down to the water around 10:00 a.m., where they mostly just hung around and talked in small groups. When the water warmed up a bit, students and teachers took rides in the kayaks and canoes, or they just played a little beach volleyball. Dad and the counselors had apparently set up a net the day before, which I was both surprised and happy to see. Everyone seemed to enjoy the food that Maria and I had made for the picnic, though I did make a mental note to ask Dad about getting a grill for the following summer; I really missed the hotdogs and hamburgers from my outings back home with my friends. After lunch, some of the boys stayed for a while to continue relaxing in the sun, and some disappeared back to their rooms. All in all, I think it went over very well.

On Sunday morning, only Mike, four students, and one of the other counselors showed up to join us on the trail. I was a little disappointed by the low turnout at first. But then I remembered how much I liked to sleep in on Sunday mornings back home, so I could not really judge the other boys. It was a little cooler out than the day before, so it was perfect for a hike, as it would keep people moving along.

When we got to the cemetery, Diego gave a little talk about the leper colony and shared some of the details he had learned. After that, we all walked to the stone foundations and sat down for a midmorning snack I had brought along. While we ate, I gave a little talk about the doctor and the staff who had set up the colony along with some background about the atmosphere at the time it was developed. The group was quiet and respectful, which I appreciated. Since the path back to the compound was clearly laid out, we gave everyone the freedom to head back whenever they wanted, though one of the counselors stayed back until the end to make sure everyone got back safely.

Franklin and I had almost finished our planning for the music and game nights. We decided they would occur twice a week, on Wednesdays and Fridays from 7:00 to 9:00 p.m. Most of the evening sessions were over by then. I had tried to talk Dad into extending the hours to 10:00 p.m. on Friday at least, but he insisted on keeping the time we had originally set.

On Sunday night, as I was heading off to my room after dinner, Dad approached me and asked if he could talk to me for a moment in his office. I followed him in, wondering what was up.

"Julia," he said, "I know how interested you are in the leper colony that was here. I have just learned that the librarian on Cuttyhunk Island is an expert on it. How do you feel about taking the ferry over there for the day next Saturday and meeting with her? I thought it would really help you with your notes for your paper."

"Wow, Dad, I would love that! Do you think Diego could come also? He is just as interested in the colony as I am," I asked hopefully.

"I'm not sure, Julia, because it would probably look like special privileges, and I try to keep everything fair here. Let me think about it," he said thoughtfully. "Maybe if I opened the invite to all interested students… and, of course, a counselor would have to go along also.

Chapter 15

I was super excited. Dad had decided to open the invitation for next Saturday to any of the boys who had shown an interest in the leper colony. In addition to Diego, that also likely meant the four boys who had come with us on the hike the previous weekend. However, when those boys heard that they could come but would have to spend the entire time in the library, they all decided not to give up their whole Saturday for the trip. That left just me, Diego, and Mike going by ourselves.

I still had the whole week ahead before we were going, which was enough time to prepare my list of questions that I would ask the librarian who we were meeting with. Meanwhile, I also still had my daily activities to oversee, including the music and game nights, which were starting this week.

On Tuesday afternoon, Diego and I led a hike on the southern trail that we both had taken previously. Our plan was to go as far as the water hole, where we would rest and have a snack break before heading back. This time five of the boys had showed up to join us, and the afternoon went great. Diego took the lead while I walked in the middle of the group, and Mike took the back. He was interested in seeing more of the island since he had such little time to explore.

We reached our destination in about an hour and a half. The boys splashed each other and waded in the clear water. After a snack break, we headed back to the compound. This time, we let them go ahead of us, with Mike in the lead and Diego and I following close behind.

After walking for a while on the path, with the boys far enough ahead of us, he took my hand as we walked. "Are you looking forward to going to Cuttyhunk Island this Saturday?" he asked without looking at me.

"Yes, for sure. How about you?" I answered, looking up at him.

"It should be fun. I hope we get a little time to also explore that island a bit, too. I only got to see the health center and the police station when I was there before. From what I've read, it's not that much bigger than this island, but it has a population of over 400 in the summer."

Why didn't it surprise me that he had already done more research on the island we were going to be visiting than I had? I thought for a moment and said, "I could ask Dad if we could take along a picnic and do a little exploring while we're there. It could maybe be a midafternoon break? I'm sure Mrs. Drake, the librarian, won't be interested in meeting with us for the entire time," I added hopefully. I decided to wait and pick a good time to ask Dad about this. I did not want to push my luck too far, and I was just excited about getting to go there regardless.

The first music and game night went off well after a shaky start. At first, the boys just milled around the room, looking uncomfortable while Franklin got the music going. They started to warm up a bit when I uncovered the cupcakes Maria and I had baked that day. I put them out along with a pitcher of lemonade, and most of the guys finally sat down in the chairs we had set around the room. Even though most of them stared at their phones the whole time—a treat they were afforded on music and game nights—and no one touched any of the games or the cards I had laid out, I still felt the evening was a success. Most of the boys and two of the interns stayed until the end of the night. I thanked Franklin for helping me and setting up the music. Though he just shrugged his shoulders, I feel he was pleased also.

I walked back to the dorm with the others. I then lingered outside with Diego before entering for the night. "You were stuck on your phone most of the night. Checking texts?" I asked. "Anything important going on?"

We had never talked about our friends or possible relationships from back home, and I was beginning to wonder if Diego had left a girlfriend back in New York. He did not answer me right away but eventually said, "Not much."

Hoping to get him to open up a bit more, I decided to mention my "breakup" before coming to the island. "Yeah, I was seeing this boy named Craig, but we broke up right before I came here."

He looked down at me and grinned. "So, you're hoping to get me to share my past loves with you?"

Furious that he always seemed to be able to see through me, I added briskly, "Not at all… just making conversation. How did you think the night went?" I added quickly to change the subject.

"It was fine," he said distractedly. "Maybe on Friday night I'll set up a card game. Do you think you can find some coins or tokens we could use?"

"Good idea. Let me look around tomorrow and see what I can find."

We stood there for another minute, just looking at one another, until one of the counselors opened the door to the building and beckoned us in. *Drats!* I thought. *I was sure we were just about to have our first kiss!* I guess I forgot that "big brother" was always watching us here. I then said goodnight to Diego and walked to my room.

The next morning at breakfast, I asked Dad about any loose change or tokens we could use for card games. He did not think money was a good idea (surprise, surprise), but he did suggest looking in the craft area for buttons or shells or rocks. Why didn't I think of that? After working with Mike that morning, I went through the cabinets again and came upon a box of buttons, a box of small toenail shells, and a bag of nuts and bolts. These would have to do for now, but I did make a mental note of collecting coins to bring next summer in order to make the betting a little more interesting for the boys.

I still hadn't gotten up the nerve to ask Dad about giving us a little free time when we got to the island on Saturday. So, on Friday morning, I knocked on his office door after breakfast and was surprised to catch him by himself in there. He looked worried about something, but I knew better than to ask about it. I also decided that then was not a good time to bring up our trip tomorrow.

"What's up, Julia?" he asked. "Are you all set for your adventure tomorrow? The weather looks like it's going to be great."

"Yes, I have all my questions written out, and I'm looking forward to going," I answered. "How are you doing, Dad?"

"I'm fine," he responded. "I wish I could go with you also. I could use the break."

"Is there a problem I can help with or just listen to?" I asked.

"Just some money issues, Julia. Nothing to worry about for this year. A couple of my backers are hesitant about donating again, though, and I'm trying to figure a way to let them know how much we are achieving here."

I thought for a minute and blurted out, "I have an idea Dad. How about I share with them my journals and my storyline about how important this project is and how much dedication it took to make it happen? They could also learn how your program relates to the history of this island. Maybe we could use the subject of my journal writings to promote your vision, Dad, and we can highlight how much your contributors help in this cause. That way they can see how important what you're doing here is and use that for their own advertising advantage."

He looked up to me, somewhat surprised, and said, "Actually, Julia... something like that could actually work. If you don't mind, I could have you coordinate your work with Matt, our intern from NYU, and maybe together you guys could come up with a release that would encourage them to continue donating."

Happy to see his spirits lifted, I quickly agreed to the idea and reviewed my schedule for the following week with him so that he could set up some time for Matt and me to get together.

I then decided to ask him the question I had come for. "Dad, quick question. Do you think I could pack a picnic lunch for tomorrow, and we could take an hour break from the library while we're at Cuttyhunk for a little tour of the island?"

I could tell his mind was already on to other things, but he did respond by saying, "Sure, that shouldn't be a problem. Make sure you make enough for the three of you."

Oh well, I thought, *I guess that's better than not being able to wander at all.*

Chapter 16

On Saturday morning, Diego, Mike and I helped unload the weekly food off the ferry before we boarded to go off for the day. It was already sunny and warm, but there was a nice cool breeze on the water. It took about forty-five minutes before we entered a beautiful, protected harbor full of boats of all sizes. After being on our little deserted island for five weeks, this place looked like a busy metropolis.

We pulled into the dock and men jumped on the ferry to help unload the supplies that were being dropped off there. One of the mates on the ship informed us that they would be docked there for six hours before heading back to the mainland. They would drop us off back on Penikese on the way back if we were here on time. We made a mental note to get back to the dock in plenty of time.

The island was picturesque, with tiny shops and quaint clapboard houses surrounded by wild gardens. Tourists gathered on the dock and were looking around for directions, just like we were. We asked a few people walking by how to find the library, but they all seemed unsure as well. There was only one road heading up a slight incline away from the shore, so we decided to follow it. There were only a few utility trucks that seemed to be active on the island's roads, along with several golf carts that kept zooming by us.

After walking for a few minutes, a woman in a cart stopped and asked us if we needed help. We knew right away that she was a "townie," with her weather-worn look, crazy hat, and high-water boots. She had a bucket of fish in the back of the cart, which looked like it had just been caught. She gave us directions to the local library and offered us a ride in her cart.

We politely declined, saying we were up for the walk and that it did not appear to be too far away. She followed along with us for a while, chatting away about the island and how much it changes when all the "summer people" invade it.

We got to the library around 10:00 a.m., which was just about when it was scheduled to open. The building itself was tucked between two other small and similar-looking buildings, which were apparently the town hall and the historical society. We entered the little brick building and were greeted by a small woman with a friendly smile, who immediately left her desk and came toward us. She introduced herself as Mrs. Drake.

Mrs. Drake led us into a small office off the main desk and told us to make ourselves comfortable. She said she was still waiting for her assistant to come so that she could give her some directions before she met with us. As she was leaving the office, Mrs. Drake pointed out some research articles and pictures she had laid out for us, and she told us to feel free to peruse them while we waited. Some of the pictures and articles were ones I had seen online, but others were not, so I dug right in, soaking up the new information.

When Mrs. Drake came back in the room, she smiled and asked if we wanted any water or coffee. When we declined, she sat down at the table with us and asked us about ourselves and what brought on the interest in the colony. I explained a little about Dad's program on Penikese and what he was trying to do there. I told her how Diego and I had discovered the small graveyard while we were exploring and how our interest was piqued from there.

We found out that Mrs. Drake had been researching the leper colony for a few years now and was still learning new facts about it. Some of the information she proceeded to tell us we already knew, but she did interject some additional facts and sentiments that were new to us.

When she spoke, it was with deep emotion and sincerity. "Penikese's leper colony was running for sixteen years before it was closed and the residents were moved to a federal leprosarium in Louisiana," she informed us. "There was a total of thirty-six known patients who lived there over the years. The colony was run by a humanitarian doctor and his wife, who worked hard to make the lives of the patients bearable. They worked with the lepers to build the little houses and the gardens that surrounded them. Dr. Parker and his wife, Marion, provided them with the special foods they requested, as many of them were new immigrants to our country. They set up paying jobs for them to make money in order to purchase items on the mainland. The patients kept busy farming and landscaping their surroundings, and it gave them some meaning to their lives while they were there."

"Dr. Parker only hired staff who were sympathetic and helpful to his vision," the librarian continued. "Marion set an atmosphere of acceptance, and she provided the patients with radios, record players, books, and magazines. She also tried to provide religious services herself until she finally convinced a clergyman to come and work with them."

Mrs. Drake went on to tell us the story of a sixteen-year-old boy who developed the illness and came to the island with his mother in 1912. He was handy with two-way radios, so he set up a communication system with the mainland, other islands, and passing ships, which gave the patients the ability to communicate with the outside world.

After spending about two hours with us and recommending several books we could order or download on the subject, Mrs. Drake got up to close the meeting. She told us she was extremely impressed that the three of us were interested in this history and wished us the best with our continued research. We thanked her, exchanged email information, and walked out feeling overwhelmed with emotion—and very much in need of a break and food.

We told Mike our plans about hiking to the top of the hill; we had learned from our local guide earlier that there was a lookout area from which you could see the whole island as well as the surrounding sights. Mike, however, surprised us by saying he was going to meet a friend he knew on the island and have lunch with her. I wondered if he had told Dad that, but I was not about to question him now. We agreed to meet back at the dock right before 3:00, and he then walked down the hill toward the dock while Diego and I headed to the lookout in the opposite direction.

It was a beautiful walk to the top of the hill, and we stopped often to look over the little stone walls and out toward the ocean. We ran into other tourists who were doing the same, and each time we did it surprised me to see other people enjoying themselves. It had been a while since I did normal things with other smiling people around, and it felt good. We made it to the lookout and climbed up to the top. From there, we had a panoramic view of Cuttyhunk and the other islands in the distance. It was breathtaking, and we just stood there staring for a while before Diego pointed to an island north of where we were.

"That's Penikese," he said. "From here it looks so close, almost like we could swim there."

The lookout was getting crowded, so we decided to take another path south of the tower toward the other side of the island. This trail was a lot less crowded, and the views were even more spectacular. When we came to a clearing, we stopped and sat on our sweatshirts, and I began to unload the lunch I had packed—sandwiches, fresh tomatoes from our garden, and homemade brownies.

After lunch, we laid back on our shirts and closed our eyes. It was so quiet and peaceful here; I did not want to move at all. Diego must have felt the same since he was as still as I was. After a while, I thought he might have fallen asleep when suddenly I felt his hand reach for mine in the grass. I smiled to myself and just enjoyed laying there with him in the sunshine.

I must have dozed off a bit, because when I opened my eyes Diego was just leaning on his elbows looking down at me. My heart did that flip thing as I looked into those dark eyes of his, and I smiled up at him.

"What are you looking at?" I said, grinning at him.

"You're pretty cute when you're sleeping," he answered.

He then bent down toward me, still staring intensely, and touched his lips lightly to mine. My heart was beating like crazy as I returned his kiss. Suddenly, he backed away and sat up.

"I think we should be heading back now," he said quite abruptly before starting to pack up our stuff.

Confused and not knowing what to say, I got up also and finished repacking my bag. We headed down the hill together, but this time we did not walk as close or stop to appreciate the scenery. *Why are boys so confusing?* I thought to myself as we approached the dock.

Mike was already there, eating an ice cream cone happily while awaiting our return. We boarded the ferry early, and Mike proceeded to tell us all about his afternoon with his friend. I guess he did not notice how quiet Diego and I had become since we had parted ways.

Chapter 17

Diego did not talk to me or look at me all the way back to Penikese. He sat in the corner on the ferry and slept, so I tried to do the same. When we got back to the compound, Dad met us and walked back to the main building with me. He was full of questions about what I had learned and anxious to hear about our whole day. I was quite tired, but I tried to fill him in with as much enthusiasm as I could. I told him as I was anxious to go back to my room and jot some notes down, so I made a quick sandwich in the kitchen and escaped to the dorm.

The next morning was another picnic day, but it did not go over quite as well as the first one. It was cooler and cloudy, so no one was too enthusiastic about going in the water or hanging out on the shore. The subs and potato salad that Maria brought were a big success. However, right after everyone ate, they started dispersing back to their rooms.

I took the opportunity to meet up with Matt during the picnic in order to continue our talk from the previous week about converting my paper to help Dad's cause. We sat a little far away from the others so we could talk about what our plan of action would be. He seemed impressed at the direction of my paper and gave a few ideas about how he could turn it into a press release. We agreed to meet the following afternoon in Dad's office to put our ideas down in writing.

Diego hadn't joined the picnic until the very end, and when he arrived, I was already in conference with Matt. He looked over at us for a moment and then sat down with a few of the boys, who were just finishing up their lunch. After a while, I walked over to say hello, but when I did, he got up and walked in the opposite direction. I scanned my brain again, as I had done all night long, wondering about what exactly I had done to tick him off.

I was determined to ignore his behavior but found myself following him down to the beach instead. "What's up, Diego?"

"Nothing," he answered. "I just need some time to myself."

"Fine," I said. "Does that mean you can't even say hello to me?"

"Hello," he said moodily. "I see you found a new friend to hang out with... you and college boy fit together well."

Surprised and a bit ticked by his attitude, I just stood there looking at him for a moment. He was always the confident one who did not seem bothered or upset by anything here. Finally, I said, "Dad asked me to work with Matt on a project for the school. We're coordinating my paper with an advertising pitch which Dad can hopefully use to raise some money for the program next year. You know a lot about my topic also. Maybe I could ask Dad if you could help us?"

"No thanks," he said quickly. "Sounds like a project perfect for you and the college dude."

He stormed off, leaving me in a huff before heading up the hill to the compound. If that was how he was going to be, I was not going to let it spoil my last few weeks here. Maybe I only imagined our connection. I was "famous" for that according to Meg... but, somehow, I knew this was different. I decided to give him time to cool off and eventually— hopefully—he'd let me know what was really bothering him.

Luckily, the next week sped quickly by, so I did not have too much time to worry about Diego. Between my regular obligations in the activity shed, helping Mike with the water sports, running the music and game nights with Franklin, and meeting daily with Matt to work on our project, I did not have much free time to myself.

Diego did not bother even coming to our music and game night on Wednesday, but Franklin and I were pleased with the turnout. We were even able to get a couple of card games going with the buttons and shells I had found. I saw Jake sitting by himself playing with his phone, so I walked over and sat down next to him. He and Diego had become close since the water incident, so if anyone had an idea what was going on with him, it would be Jake.

"How's it going, Jake?" I asked.

"Not bad. How are things with you?" he responded.

"Pretty good," I answered, wondering how I could broach the subject of Diego with him. I decided to just be direct and asked him, "Any ideas what's up with Diego? He's been ignoring me lately and acting kind of moody."

"I think he has a lot on his mind, Julia," he answered thoughtfully. "We all do. Being here has been great but remember, we all must go home to our old lives after this. And none of us are certain what that means day by day."

I guess I just was making Diego's problem about me and not even considering that he must be worried about his life when he gets back to the city.

I was just about to tell Jake I understood when he added, "Plus, I think he really likes you, Julia, and it's probably bugging him that the summer is almost over, and he won't be seeing you again."

"I'm going to miss all you guys, Jake," I responded. "I'm hoping to stay in touch with you over the coming year if that works for you?"

With a better understanding of what was going on with Diego, I made the decision to swallow my pride and seek him out the next chance I could. That opportunity came the next morning down by the water. I arrived early, hoping to run into him before the boys showed up for their lessons. And there he was, putting out the floats and swim supplies.

I approached him hesitantly. "Hi, are you talking to me today?"

He just looked at me and said, "How's your project with the college boy going?"

"Is that what this is all about Diego? Are you jealous of Matt? For your information, he spends half the time we are meeting on the project telling me about his girlfriend back home and how great she is. This is more than that Diego. You've been mad at me since our picnic on Cuttyhunk. Are you just trying to brush me off because I'm not an experienced kisser?" I added, now getting angry myself at this whole conversation.

He grinned and said quickly, "Actually, you're a pretty good kisser."

"Then why the cold shoulder right after we kissed?" I questioned him, looking at him directly for the first time in a while.

"It dawned on me that you're going back home to your life, Julia, and I'm going to mine. We have nothing in common and no chance to continue whatever this is. I would only drag you down if we tried to see each other, and I have no idea what my year will look like when I return."

"I think you're giving up on us awfully easily, Diego. Who knows what will happen this coming year? And it's not like we can't communicate with each other; I can take trips to visit my Dad throughout the year, especially now that I'm part of his ad campaign," I said with a grin.

"That's true," he agreed. "And I can always show you parts of the city you are not familiar with. There are some neat parks and restaurants I think you would like."

"And" I added in, "there's always the library we can visit."

Diego stood up and grabbed my hand. I was hoping we were going to have our second kiss, but we heard the boys coming down the path. Disappointed, but still hopeful, we separated and started setting up for the lesson. *Maybe my last two weeks here will be good ones after all*, I thought with a smile.

Chapter 18

Before I knew it, there were only two weeks left on the island. The first week was business as usual filled with classes, sessions for the guys, and meeting with Matt to finish up our plan. Matt would continue working with Dad when they returned to New York, and I would join them when I could on my visits to the city.

Things slowed down during the last week in preparation of everyone packing up and getting ready to depart the island. Also, Dad and his staff had plans to celebrate the summer with some surprises for the boys. Thursday would be mostly a cleanup and packing day, but there would be a closing picnic down at the beach with music and special food.

At the end of the year picnic, everyone hung out until the sun had long gone down. Dad finally allowed us to have a bonfire with brush we had collected all summer long, and Franklin again provided all the music to fit the atmosphere. Diego and I stayed until the very end with the other boys, which was long after Dad and the staff had retired to their rooms. I was given the task of making sure the fire was completely out before we left, but no one seemed in a hurry to end the night.

Finally, around midnight, the boys started heading up to their rooms, and Diego and I started cleaning up what was left behind. We brought buckets of water up from the beach and put out the fire slowly. The stars were beautiful, but it suddenly felt cool standing there with the last sparks of the fire hissing. I began shivering when Diego came over and put his arms around me, and we just stood there looking up at the sky.

"It all went by so fast," I said as I hugged him back. "I wish we had more time here."

"It's been quite a summer," he responded. "I'm sorry it has to end."

"Are you nervous about going back home?" I asked.

"Not really. I'm looking forward to seeing my stepmom and getting back to school. And I'm scheduled for a visit with my dad in a couple of weeks. How about you?" he asked.

"I'll be glad to see my mom again and catch up with my friends," I answered. "It should be an interesting year at school. I have a hard schedule, but I'm excited about my paper and working on finishing it up this school year."

We held each other for a while longer, and then we had our second kiss—a *real* kiss this time. It felt natural and was beginning to deepen when I noticed blinking lights coming from the dorm.

"I guess someone stayed up for us," I said with a grimace, as we headed up the hill together.

On Friday, Dad had hired a small yacht for the entire staff and the boys to go cruising around the islands in the area. Maria and I were busy preparing all the special foods we would bring along, trying hard to use up all the spare stuff we had left. It would be a day of feasting and fun for sure. The small yacht was owned by a friend of Dad's who summered in the area. He and two of his crew brought us all around the surrounding islands, giving us a quick history of each one. Later in the day, several of the boys had lessons in ocean fishing while trolling behind the boat as we meandered around. Diego took an interest in running the ship, so the captain let him hang out in the helm to learn the ins and outs of boat maneuvering.

After Maria and I put out the last meal and cleaned up the galley, I went to the top deck to sunbathe. I had almost fallen asleep when Dad approached and said, "Quite a day, huh? It went much better than I expected."

"It's been great, Dad." I responded. "The whole summer has been a learning experience I won't forget."

"You've been a wonderful help, Julia. I'm hoping you'll think about coming back next year if I can make this happen again."

"I'm sure you will, Dad. It's amazing what you've accomplished here. I'll think about it. Though with college approaching quickly, I should start thinking about getting a paid job."

"True, but maybe I can work something out so I can start paying my interns as well. And working here will look impressive on your college resume," he added.

I hadn't thought about that, and I would like to spend another summer here with Dad—even though it would not be the same without Diego here as well. "What about Diego, Dad? Do you think there could be a job for him here next year also?"

"Let's not get ahead of ourselves, Julia," he quickly cut me off. "There's a lot going on in Diego's life right now, and I'm going to try to be there for him as much as I can, but I have a lot of boys I'm working with and want to help."

"I know Dad," I conceded, "But he was such a big help here. He's not exactly like all the other boys, is he?"

"I admit that, Julia, but like I said before, I had to pull some strings to make him fit the program. I did want to get him away from his home for the summer, as his stepbrother is not a great influence on him."

"But won't he still have that when he goes back now, Dad?" I asked worried.

"From what I have gathered from here, his brother is now living elsewhere with friends in a different part of the city. If that situation stays the same, then things will be a lot better for Diego when he goes home. I shouldn't be telling you any of this Julia, but I know you do care about him and want what's best for him."

"I do, Dad, and we plan to see each other a bit when I come to visit you in the city," I offered hesitantly. "I hope you're not going to have a problem with that."

"Why don't we just cross that bridge when it comes, Julia?" he said. "You have a remarkably busy year ahead of you. Junior year is the most important college preparatory year. And between courses and social obligations, I'm sure you'll have your hands full."

I knew I was being dismissed. This is something Dad did when he was done talking about a subject, so I let it go.

We got back to the shore just as the sun was setting and lumbered back to our rooms, tired and relaxed from a full day on the water. The next day would be a busy one with closing the camp and doing our final packing before heading out on Sunday morning.

Chapter 19

On Saturday morning, everyone was assigned a job to do as we all worked along with the counselors to close the camp. Diego and I worked with Mike in the shed, storing everything safely for the following year. It seemed like only a short time ago I had ventured in here to scout the place out.

The ferry would be picking all of us up the following morning to bring us back to the mainland. From there, most of us would be boarding a bus heading to New York. The boys would be met by their families, and Dad and I would head to his apartment for a day before Mom came to pick me up.

On Saturday evening, some of the boys and I exchanged email information as we listened to the music Franklin had arranged for us. The guys were used to Diego and I being together by now, and they did not even kid us as we sat close together on the couch holding hands.

After the boys had all left to finish their packing, Diego and I walked out front again for one last look at the ocean at night. I knew in my heart it would not be the end for us and, somehow, I think he did too. We both had a big year ahead, but this summer on Penikese Island would always be with us. And, who knows, perhaps next summer would be even better?

The ferry picked us up early Sunday morning to bring us to the mainland. I stayed on the top deck with Diego even though it was windy and cold. We wanted to spend every minute together before we had to part. Dad had hired a bus to pick us all up at the ferry station. Diego and I sat at the back of the bus, and other than stopping for a quick lunch, we just sat quietly holding hands. Dad sat in the middle of the bus with Ann, conversing quietly with her and looking happy and comfortable. I must have fallen asleep after a while, because before I knew it, we were at the bus station in New York.

Diego and I got off last, and I noticed he was looking around as other families were uniting. Finally, I saw him walk off toward a tall woman with a big smile on her face.

I walked off to look for Dad, but he was busy talking to several of the families who had come to collect their sons. I approached some of the guys for one last goodbye and then stood off to the side waiting for Dad to finish up.

As I waited, I felt so proud of Dad and could see the excitement on his face as he talked to the various family members of the boys. The family units were not the ones I was used to in Connecticut, even though many of my friends also came from broken families. Some of the relatives who came to pick up their boy were obviously grandparents or even older siblings. But everyone there seemed interested in how the summer went, and they were excited about seeing their loved ones.

I looked around for Diego, hoping he hadn't left yet, but I could not find him. Dad was finally walking toward me, so I went to pick up my bags, not sure how I was feeling. Dad pointed behind me, and there was Diego standing with his stepmom. I walked up to them, and Diego introduced me to her.

"It's nice to meet you, Mrs. Costa," I said as I held out my hand.

"You can call me Beth," she responded. I was surprised to see that she did not look old enough to be a mom. "I've heard a lot about you from Diego," she continued. "I think you made his stay on the island a lot more enjoyable."

I smiled and said, "That goes both ways. We have a lot in common and hope to see each other over the school year."

She looked surprised by that but did not respond further. After one last quick hug from Diego, he went to collect his bags while Dad and Beth talked quietly. After they left, Dad and I walked out front, and the overwhelming feeling of how different everything was going to be finally hit me. It would take some time to get used to this noise again. We took a cab back to his apartment. After ordering pizza for dinner, I told Dad I was exhausted and headed to bed.

I lay in bed for a while, just going over everything in my mind and trying to think ahead with some excitement for the coming year. When I realized I could not possibly sleep, I texted Diego to see if he were still up. He answered right away, and after going back and forth for a while, we signed off. I tried to sleep again but was still too restless. Finally, I jumped out of bed and opened my laptop. Suddenly, I felt calm and optimistic as I started to rewrite my paper. I had so much to say and pass on about my island experience and how it had affected me. Then, the title came to me:

Penikese: An Island of Hope and Love
Past and Present

Chapter 20

Why did I schedule so many classes into this school year? I thought I was so smart by loading up my junior year with AP classes. But little did I realize that there would be no extra time for anything but studying and reports and presentations.

Diego and I talked a few times a week when school first started. We made plans for what we would do when I got to New York, and we shared stories of classes and the challenges of starting a new school year. Diego was a senior and taking his first AP classes, and I was proud of how he was doing. I had learned the summer before how smart he was, so, I, along with Dad, encouraged him to try two of the newly added AP classes that had just been introduced at his school.

It was not all my fault that I only got to New York one time that fall. The first time I tried, two of my teachers decided to push a last-minute assignment on me, and I needed the whole weekend to get them done. It was still my goal to graduate as the top student in the 2018 class and blowing off those assignments was not going to get me there. Another time— when I had a free weekend—I found out that he and Ann had plans to go off for a getaway at the same time.

I finally got to the city for Thanksgiving weekend, and I had a wonderful time with my dad and Ann. I got to see some of my friends from camp as well. Jake and Franklin met me at a park downtown, and we walked around and talked about what they were up to. Later, we met up with Diego after he got off work, and we had pizza at a restaurant he suggested not far from where we met up. It was great seeing them all, and when Jake and Franklin headed home, Diego walked me back to Dad's apartment. I told him I could go by myself on the train, but he said it would give us more time to talk.

I was happy walking beside him, and many of the feelings I had for him that summer started to float back into my heart. He did not reach for my hand like I was hoping he would, but we did walk close together while chatting about school, jobs, and the approaching holiday season. I told him I would not be able to return for Christmas, as Dad was coming to Connecticut instead this year. That was a ritual that occurred for the past few years since my parents' amicable divorce, and I always looked forward to all of us being together. I had been surprised when Dad mentioned that he was still coming, thinking that perhaps he would prefer to stay in the city and have Christmas with Ann.

I had finally told my best friend Meg about Diego. I was hesitant at first knowing she would be skeptical of him. Meg likes to point out to me that I'm always jumping to conclusions with boys, and that I "really don't know how to read them at all." I was anxious to be able to tell Meg all about reconnecting with Diego on this visit.

Just as we were approaching Dad's apartment building and I was about to invite Diego in, he grabbed my hand. But this felt different, and I was not completely surprised when Diego said, "Julia, we've got to talk."

"I thought we were talking," I responded a bit slowly.

"I mentioned my friend Sophia to you the last time we were talking—the one in both of my AP classes?"

"Yes, you said she was really smart and helping you with some of the work. I told you I bet you were helping her even more," I answered quickly, anxious to hear what this was about.

"Well, our school is having a Christmas dance in a couple of weeks and she asked me to go with her. I just wanted to let you know about that," he continued. "Not like a date or anything… but most of the kids are going in couples, so I thought it would be more fun if we did also."

"So, why are you telling me this?" I asked nonchalantly, though my heart was beating hard and I was afraid I would do something stupid—like cry.

"Just so you know, Julia. I'm sure you have dances and social things coming up at your school, and I definitely want you to be able to attend them also."

"Yeah, whatever," I said casually. "I'm not really into those things. I've got a lot of work and projects that I'm involved in, and I haven't thought much about what's going on socially at the school."

That was not entirely true, though. There was a dance coming up, and though some of my friends were going with dates, most of them were going in a group altogether. I have been purposely avoiding one boy who I think wanted to ask me, because I thought it would be a lot more fun going with my girlfriends. I guess there were not the same type of dynamics at Diego's school, or maybe he was just the type that would prefer to go with a date. *He probably likes her anyway*, I thought, *and I bet she's super cute.*

I was working myself into a major funk when I quickly said, "Well, I have to go Diego. It was great to see you. Make sure you write and let me know how the dance goes." Before he could respond, I ran up the stairs and let myself into the apartment.

Great, I thought, *now I'm going to hear from Meg, again, how I jumped to conclusions about Diego and how he really wasn't that "into me" after all*. Hoping Dad was too busy to notice that I was back, I quietly went up to my room and shut the door. Unfortunately, however, he did hear me, and a few minutes later there was a knock.

"Hi, Hun, how was your day? Did you meet up with all your friends?" Before I could answer, he continued, "I hadn't heard from you since you made it to the park. Remember the deal? You were supposed to text me every two hours or so to let me know where you were."

"Sorry, Dad," I answered. "We were so busy and having such a good time that I forgot. I won't forget next time... though I don't think I'll be coming back again too soon. My workload is really getting out of control, and I'm trying to keep up with that and all my other commitments this year."

I was not entirely lying either. To make my junior year resume look good, I had signed up for the yearbook committee, the tutoring club, and ran for class treasurer, which I won.

"I did think you were overextending a bit, Julia. Do you think you should drop some of your commitments?"

"No, I can handle them fine. I was just letting you know that I won't be back for a while. I'm really glad that you're coming for Christmas, though, and so is Mom."

The next day, I was scheduled to meet up with Matt at Dad's office in the city. He was now a junior at NYU, but he still worked with Dad as a volunteer. Since it was my idea to use the premise of my paper as an advertising pitch for Dad's camp, I had been staying connected to the project. We were almost done with the presentation, and it was Dad's plan to take it around the country to instill confidence in his program. I felt strongly that the camp was an incredibly unique concept, and it was one that proved successful, at least on a smaller scale, the summer before.

All ten boys seemed to get a lot out of the camp that summer, and when I asked Dad for follow-up details on some of them, he admitted that at least eight of the boys have succeeded in starting to turn their lives around. He would not elaborate on the two who did not, other than that they were still both a "work in progress." I knew better than to press him further on that topic.

I was excited to see the final copy of the program, and I was not disappointed when Matt handed me a copy of the pamphlet that read:

Penikese Island Experiment:
A Juvenile Court System Alternative
A Program Based on Trust, Therapy, and Second Chances

Dr. Philip Cooper
(Licensed Clinical Psychologist)

Chapter 21

Before I knew it, Christmas was almost here. I tried to get excited, but this year it just was not happening. Studying for finals took up most of my time, though I did get out of taking two of them because of my high averages. I did not have too much to do on the yearbook committee, but I did have to attend the senior meetings in preparation for next year. That was kind of fun, and one of the senior boys on the committee, Sam, was especially helpful. He always saved a seat for me when I came in and walked me to my car after the meetings. Meg said it was because he was interested in me, but there were so many pretty senior girls who were also in the meeting that I could not quite buy that.

One afternoon, after a yearbook meeting, Sam hung around even after we got to my car. He was talking about his college choices, and I was interested as to why he chose the ones he did. I was just about to ask him about that when he suddenly said, "So, are you going to the Christmas formal with anyone?"

"No, not really," I answered.

"You're not sure?" he said with a grin.

"Well, a bunch of us girls were going to go together, but we have no definite plans yet," I answered.

"You want to go with me?" he asked confidently.

I hesitated for just a second. My heart was not doing that flip thing it often does when I'm interested in a guy. But, on the other hand...

"Sure," I said with a smile. "That sounds like fun."

"Great, I'll call you next week and set up plans," he said as he waved goodbye and headed toward his own car.

I had mixed feeling about the whole thing. In a way, I was looking forward to going with my friends and the plans we had beforehand. We were all planning to meet at a friend's house to order food and then help each other get ready before the dance. But at the same time, I remembered Diego's "dance date," and I thought it would be fun to casually mention Sam in our next conversation. We had spoken a few times since I'd seen him in November. All the calls had been initiated by him, and most of the time I only had a few minutes to talk. His dance never came up in conversation and he never mentioned Sofia again. It was almost like he was avoiding bringing her up.

When I told Meg about Sam asking me to the Christmas formal, I did not get the reaction I expected from her. Usually, we encourage each other in our dating experiences, but right now she was between boyfriends, and we had been hanging out more often on the weekends because of that.

"But, Julia, this will probably be our last time we'll be able to go to a dance as a group. We had so many fun things planned. Next year, I'm sure we'll all be going with dates. But this was the perfect opportunity to go and just have a blast together," she added in a pleading voice.

Meg gets overly dramatic when she is trying to make a point, and she did not disappoint this time. I explained that Sam and I would also be going as friends and that we could join the group when we got to the dance.

"Oh, sure," she added with a sigh, "I'm so convinced that he's going to hang around with a bunch of juniors at his last Christmas dance. Sam is pretty popular, so I'm betting you'll be going in a limo with a bunch of the in-crowd he hangs around with."

Again, I knew she was exaggerating, but I did not argue with her. Sam did seem to have a nice group of friends, but they were not the group that Meg was referring to. Many of his friends were in my advanced classes, and I was sure I would fit in with them without a problem.

Not one to be ignored, Meg continued, "You're just doing this because Diego is taking a date to his dance. Admit it, Julia."

"I don't know, Meg," I said honestly. "That may be part of the reason, I'll admit, but it's not the whole reason. I like Sam and feel comfortable with him. He may be a senior, but he doesn't put anyone down, and he is super excited about leaving for college next year. I like hearing about his options, and I am learning a lot about how to start the process and narrow down choices."

"Oh wow! That sounds so romantic!" Meg said sarcastically.

I chose not to encourage her anymore and just said I had to go and help my mom, who had just come home. Diego did not call or text that week or the following weekend, and I was "definitely not" going to call him, I thought, as I pressed on his number on my phone.

"Hey," he said. "How are you?"

"Fine," I answered. "How have you been?"

"Busy with work and school. I got to see my dad this week, though. Monday was the day that his case came up for consideration, and I got to sit in at the hearing with my stepmom. Your dad met us there and sat with us."

I had completely forgotten about that appointment coming up and felt guilty that I had been avoiding him when he was going through that.

"How did it go?" I asked with concern. I could pretend that was the reason I had called but doing so four days after it occurred did not make me seem too interested. "I'm really sorry I didn't call you earlier."

"I think it went well. An officer at the prison spoke up for my dad, and he said he was a model prisoner. And best of all, your dad spoke to his character, too. Now, we just need to wait and see what the board decides on his case." After a short moment of silence, he asked, "What's new with you?"

Well, I could not really slip in my date now or make it fit into the conversation, so I just told him about my finals and how all my meetings were going. I wanted to ask him about his upcoming dance and when exactly it was going to be, but I did not know how to broach it. Finally, I just said I had to go, and I asked him to call me when his dad's verdict came in. He said he would. Then, after another awkward silence, he said goodbye and hung up.

I felt worse than I had for a while after that and decided to call my dad, who could usually cheer me up a bit. Unfortunately, he did not answer his phone, and I started to feel dejected all around when my mom knocked on my door.

"Want to go out for sushi tonight?" she asked hopefully.

"I've got too much work tonight, Mom," I answered. "Perhaps this weekend I'll have some free time. By the way, I'm going to the Christmas formal with my friend Sam next week. Want to help me find a new dress to wear?"

"Sure, Hun, that's sounds great," Mom said excitedly. "Let's go shopping Saturday, and then we can stop for lunch or an early dinner."

"I just thought I'd find something online, Mom," I responded quickly. But when I saw her face, I quickly added, "But I guess I can go on Saturday as long as we don't take all day to find one."

"Super," she said. "Then it's a date!"

Mom and I did have a great time shopping on Saturday, and we even spent time getting our nails done and grabbed lunch together. By the time I got home, I was much more excited about the dance, and I was surprised I still hadn't heard from Sam about the specific details. But on Monday morning, he did approach me in the hallway at school and apologized for not calling me yet.

"Sorry I haven't called you, Julia, but I've been super busy. How's does seven work for you on Friday night? We'll stop and grab something to eat with a few of my friends and then head to the dance?"

"That works," I said. "Do you need my address?"

"I'll find you," he said with a grin and then headed off toward his next class.

Chapter 22

Friday night came quickly, and I was all dressed and ready to go when Sam picked me up. We had a great time with his friends at dinner, which was held in a nicer place than I expected. I felt comfortable with them, and they accepted me as if I were one of their crowd. We got to the dance a little later than many others, but that was to be expected from a bunch of seniors who said they were just going to "stop by."

After settling at a table, I went over to say hello to my group of friends, and they were all happy to see me. Meg, however, still appeared a little standoffish when I complimented her dress. I danced with Sam a few times, but he mostly just sat around a talked with friends about their future endeavors, so I went to join my girlfriends and danced with them much of the night.

All in all, I had a good time at the dance, and when Sam dropped me off and gave me a quick kiss goodnight, I thanked him sincerely. "I really had a nice time tonight, Sam. Thanks for inviting me."

"Yeah, I wondered when you kept leaving to join your girlfriends, Julia," he replied with a grin. "My friends are kind of over the whole dance thing. I'm even surprised we all stayed as long as we did."

"I understand, Sam," I went on quickly. "I'll probably be the same way next year when my college prospects get more defined."

He gave me a quick hug and said, "See you soon. I'm off next week for my last college visit. I'll let you know how it goes."

I felt that we parted that night as friends, and I felt good about not having to let him know I was not interested in a continued relationship. Obviously, he felt the same, and that made things a lot easier. I called Meg the next day to see if she wanted to come over for a sleepover and hang out. She warmed up a bit and said she was waiting on a phone call but would let me know. Apparently, one of her past boyfriends was home from college and said he might give her a call if he had the time.

I knew she really liked Jack, and it was tough for her when they broke up this fall when he left for college. Part of me hoped he would not string her along and get her interested again. She did call later that day, however, saying she was free and that she would come over.

When she arrived, she seemed sad and distracted, so I decided not to ask her about Jack. She asked me about my date instead, and I was glad I could answer that I had a good time but that Sam and I were just friends.

"That's good," she said quickly. "That way you won't have to break up when he goes off to college. What do you hear from Diego these days? How did his date go?"

I was sorry I had told her about that because she had taken a few opportunities to bring it up. But I decided to answer her honestly and said, "I'm really not sure. The few times we have talked since it happened, he didn't bring it up and I didn't ask."

As it turned out, Meg and I had a really good time after that. We basically did nothing but sit around and eat pizza that Mom had ordered for us, talking and laughing between bites. I was beginning to feel like I had my old best friend back again. We even talked a bit about colleges, and I learned a lot about Meg's interests, which surprised me. Her mom was a nurse, and she was always complaining about her not being around on weekends or evenings when she needed her. That's why I was shocked to hear her say that she was thinking about getting her degree in nursing and that she hoped to work with young children.

When she asked me what I was interested in, I hesitated before saying, "I'm not sure, but I'm wondering about going into counseling like my dad. Either that or something to do with math or economics."

"Wow," she said with a grin, "that's quite a variation. I guess you'll start out in a liberal arts school so you can ponder your choices."

"That's my plan," I continued. "I'm hoping to visit NYU when I visit my dad next time. That's supposed to be a great liberal arts school."

"Are you sure that's the only reason you're thinking about that school?" Meg joked with me. I ignored her question as we sat down to watch a Christmas movie that we had both seen many times. We stayed up late and finally went to bed around 2:00 a.m.

The last three days of school before the break went by quickly, and before I knew it, we were anticipating Dad's visit for Christmas. Mom and I decorated the house and even left some ornaments for Dad to add to the tree.

It was fun having him here at Christmas—almost like old times. We had a traditional scallop dinner on Christmas Eve, one of Mom's only successful recipes, and then went out and walked around the town while looking at the lights and festivities. We stayed up late, opened presents, and played Christmas music. The next day, Dad made a big breakfast and then prepared to leave. I was a bit sad he was leaving so early on Christmas Day, but I understood why since Mom's brother and family were coming for Christmas dinner; they were not on the best of terms with Dad. Besides, I'm sure he wanted to go back to the city and spend time with Ann.

I was a bit down after he left and wondered what I would do to occupy myself with a whole week off from school. Just as I was feeling the sorriest for myself, my phone rang, and I saw that it was Diego. He asked me about my Christmas, and I asked him about his. He said his was quiet, but he said that the food his stepmom made was great and several of their relatives stopped by to visit.

"I went into the city to look at the lights and Christmas displays with a few friends," he said cheerfully. "They were great. Maybe next year you can have Christmas here and we can check them out together?"

Loving the idea, I added enthusiastically, "And we could go skating in Rockefeller Center!"

"Let's not push your luck, Julia," he said with a chuckle. "But it would be great to see you at this time of the year. Do you think you could make it happen next year?"

Happy about the fact that he was talking about next year, I just added, "We'll have to see, but I would love it also. I've never seen the city at Christmas time."

We signed off, promising to stay in touch, and I went to bed feeling not quite as lonely or bored. Mom had wanted to take me around to a few local colleges over vacation, and though they would be devoid of students, it was something different we could do together. I was determined to make the best of it and enjoy our week together.

Chapter 23

After Christmas break, things got even busier at school. I tried to get to New York a few times, but things kept getting in the way. I continued to chat with Diego about once a week, but our conversations became shorter and shorter as we had less in common to talk about. He was busy forming plans for after he graduated; he was leaning toward working for a year to save up some money for further schooling. That, of course, made sense, but it was not something I was considering doing or could relate to. Instead, I was surrounded by seniors who were just narrowing down their various choices of schools.

I did try to encourage him to take a few courses while he was taking his gap year, and he got quiet after that. Finally, he said, "Julia, you have no idea how much it costs to take 'a few courses' around here. You basically must enroll into a school part-time. I don't have the money for that, but that is apparently something you can't understand."

"Just making a suggestion, Diego, and you don't have to attack me," I said hotly. I then added that I had to get going and signed off our conversation.

We did not talk for a few weeks after that, but I was planning a trip to New York over spring break to meet up with Matt and Dad. They were about to leave for Dad's fundraising journey around the country. I was excited for them and glad that Matt was able to take a couple of weeks off to go with Dad and provide his perspective. They wanted me to go over some details again and hear my final input as well. I had also arranged to have Jake and Franklin come to Dad's office to be taped and interviewed about their experiences with the program.

Dad, of course, was perplexed when I did not involve Diego at all. "I thought he would be the perfect person to speak about the program, Julia. He's so articulate and introspective about everything. He would come off as quite convincing, I think."

"Almost too much so, Dad," I said quickly. "Do you think he really represents the typical student you are trying to help?"

"I don't think there is a 'typical' young man that gets into trouble, Julia. That is the prejudice I am trying to expel with this program."

I felt a bit embarrassed after he said that, but I did not want to share my real reason for not reaching out to Diego, so I let it go. "Maybe I'll give him a call and see if he can join us also, Dad. He's really busy trying to help his family and finishing up his schoolwork."

"Good idea, Julia. I did hear from him last week that he got a job for next year interning at an engineering firm in the city, and they were paying for him to take a few courses while he was working there. You probably knew that, though," he added, trying not to sound too judgmental.

Why do I always feel guilty when I'm dealing with Diego? I wanted to ask about how his dad's pardon was going, but I was afraid to admit that I did not know that either, so I let the conversation go after that. I did get up the nerve to call Diego a few days before I was ready to head to New York. He seemed happy to hear from me, and the conversation went better than I expected.

"So, Dad tells me you have a job prospect for the fall?"

"Yes," he said enthusiastically. "I applied for a special program for inner-city students and got an interview pretty quickly. They liked my transcript and hired me to start in September. I was hoping they wanted me over the summer, but they didn't have any spots until the fall."

"That's great news, Diego. And Dad said they would pay for a few courses toward a degree?" I asked, trying not to sound haughty.

"Yes, that's the best part. They have a grant from the government to help educate inner-city students, and they said I was a great candidate," he added excitedly.

"I'm proud of you, Diego, and I know my dad is also. What's the latest news on your dad?" I asked.

"Didn't your dad tell you? He's being released a few months early and should be out of prison by May sometime."

"That's great, Diego! No, Dad didn't mention that to me, but as you know he doesn't usually talk about his job or the people he helps in it."

After breaking the ice with Diego, I explained to him that I was coming to New York the following week to finalize our project for the camp before Dad took off on a fundraising tour. I explained that I had invited Jake and Franklin to join us to be interviewed on Saturday afternoon, and invited him to join us also.

He seemed a little taken aback by the last-minute invitation, and he added quickly that he was working but perhaps we could meet up that evening. I told him that was a great idea, and I would ask the guys if they wanted to join us also. It felt good to hang up and realize that we were still friends and on decent terms.

The trip to New York turned out to be a lot of fun. Dad had arranged for me to visit a few colleges in the city while I was there, and he seemed proud to take me around on these visits. I especially liked the openness and flexibility of NYU, and I made a mental note to add it to the top of my list for possible colleges. I got to know Ann better also, as we tried a few new restaurants with Dad and went shopping together one day. She was a bargain shopper like me, so we meshed well together. She introduced me to a few cute boutiques that I never would have walked into on my own, but they turned out to be treasures for sure.

On Saturday, we met up with Matt for breakfast and then went to Dad's office for our meeting. I could tell that Dad and Matt were excited as they showed me the whole presentation on the computer. It was their hope to use the discussion with the boys to finalize their presentation. Before the boys showed up, Matt interviewed me about the camp, and I gave my perspective on its meaning and how I believe it worked. I was able to explain what the island meant to me and how the discovery of the former leper colony helped put things in perspective. It seemed to me that the island was put there to help save and comfort people, and that became the whole concept of my thesis paper, which I went on to explain in the interview.

When the boys showed up, they seemed nervous, but Dad and Matt put them at ease right away. During the interview, Matt brought up some of the activities they participated in at the camp and asked them about what their life has been like since they returned home. It was an honest and open discussion, and neither of the boys tried to sugarcoat the reality of what their life's challenges had been before and after the camp. Franklin did end the interview with the perfect statement that surprised us all, though. "After that summer," he said, "I realized what life could be like." And after a brief hesitation, he added, "So I came back and changed a few things."

He looked like he wanted to say more but was not sure how to. It was a sincere and heartfelt statement, though, and it turned out to be the best way to end the interview. As the guys were ready to leave, I asked them if they wanted to join Diego and me later for some food and a visit. They both said to text them, and they would try to meet up with us.

I then turned to Dad and brought up the subject of working at the camp again that coming summer. He seemed happy that I brought it up and said he would love to have me there, but he was not sure how big the program would be this summer. Last year, he had been able to pay for three counselors, a nurse, two utility workers, and a cook to join us. A few of his sponsors had dropped out this year, so the program itself was hinging on the success of this fundraising trip.

I reminded him that he would not have to pay me, if he were still fine with me not making any money this coming summer. He reiterated that he thought my college resume was just as important, and he knew how good this type of work would look on it, whether it be as a volunteer or a paid worker. We spent the rest of the day visiting a museum that he wanted me to see, and then we parted ways so I could meet up with Diego at a pizza place he had mentioned. I wanted to take the subway, but Dad insisted on dropping me off in a cab, so I arrived a bit early. As I was waiting in the restaurant, I texted the boys the address of the spot we were meeting, and I then started looking at some brochures I picked up at the various colleges we visited in the area.

Chapter 24

"You look pretty serious there," Diego said while slipping into the booth across from me.

My heart did that pitter-patter thing again as I tried to say casually, "Hi… just looking over some college material I picked up with my Dad this week."

"Thinking about coming to college in the city?" he asked.

"It's a possibility, though my mom is pushing for me to go away further. She thinks it would be good for me to see another part of our country and experience life elsewhere. Though I did bring up to her that life in New York City would be quite different from our life in the Connecticut suburbs."

"What are you thinking about studying?"

"I'm not quite sure," I answered, "which is one reason why I really liked NYU, since it seems to have so many possibilities."

"I bet," he added. "And it would be great having you here in the city," he said with a grin.

It felt good to be kidding with him again, and we chatted for a while longer before Franklin walked through the door. He joined us in the booth, taking the seat next to me. He was a big guy and would not have fit very well on the other side with Diego. We all ordered pizza, and shortly after that Jake walked in with a girl. She was cute and seemed somewhat shy as Jake introduced us to his new friend, Isabel. She took the seat next to Diego, and Jake pulled up a chair from a nearby table. There was plenty of pizza and soda for everyone, so they just joined us and started eating after the waitress brought over extra plates.

We laughed and talked and reminisced about the camp experience, which Isabel kept asking questions about. Jake had repeated a grade when he returned from the camp and started taking school much more seriously, he said. He and Isabel were juniors, like I was, and she was also looking into colleges for the future. Jake brought up that he was going to go into the pipefitting business with his uncle and what great prospects it offered him. Franklin hinted around that maybe Jake could hire him someday to work for him, and we all laughed at that.

After we paid the bill, the guys and Isabel took off, and Diego offered to walk me back to my dad's place. "I'd like to go with you, Diego, but Dad made me promise that I would take a cab back after we met."

"Why don't you text him and tell him you're with me?" he suggested. "We can walk a while and then hop on the subway that gets off near his apartment."

Surprisingly, Dad agreed with the new plan, so we took off and walked through a park that Diego was familiar with. It was through several nice downtown neighborhoods that I had never seen.

"See, there are some pretty nice places in the city outside of the high-rent district," he pointed out.

During our walk, he pointed out some additional dorms and buildings at NYU that I was not even sure Dad knew about. I was surprised when he grabbed my hand for part of the walk, and I wanted to ask about whether he was still seeing Sophia, but I did not want to break the spell. After a while, it was getting harder to walk the busier streets, so we took the subway and got off near Dad's apartment. Approaching his door, I asked him if he wanted to come in, but he said he had to get back. We hugged goodbye and promised each other we would stay in touch.

"Let me know how things go with your dad," I said sincerely.

"Will do," he said. "Stay in touch."

I returned to school that spring ready to finish up my projects and start planning my summer ahead. When I told

Mom that I planned to spend another summer at the camp with Dad, she was not too thrilled about the idea.

"I really hoped we could take some college trips this summer, Julia," she pressed. "Maybe even visiting some in other states and take in the sights while we're there."

"I've more or less made up my mind that I'm going to NYU if I can get in, Mom," I retorted. "But I will apply to a few schools in other states just in case I change my mind or don't get in. I'm really interested in working with Dad again, and I think he really appreciates my help there."

Knowing better than to argue with me, but obviously not pleased, she added hesitantly, "OK, Julia, let's wait and see how Dad's fundraising trip goes, and we'll talk more after we know for sure what's happening."

It upset me to know that she was almost hoping that Dad's trip would fail. She obviously did not understand how important his work at the camp was. Then it suddenly dawned on me that I hadn't really shared my paper with Mom, and an idea popped into my mind.

"Mom, I'm presenting my college essay for my writing course next week in class. We were told that we can bring guests along for the presentation so that it would feel more like a college-speaking experience. Would you like to come and hear my talk?"

The next week in class, I was surprised that I was feeling more excited about my presentation and not at all nervous. I had spent a lot of time creating picture slides of the camp as well as the remnants of the leper colony. Mom sat in the back of the class along with a few other parents that had come to hear the presentations. One boy was ahead of me that day, and he talked about his trip the previous summer to Uruguay to help build houses for the villagers there. He also had a slideshow, and I hoped my presentation would not look too similar.

When it was time for my talk, I stood up and tried to calm my excitement and enthusiasm in order to highlight the importance of Dad's work. I presented it as "Dr. Cooper's dream project," as I did not want to stress the fact that this was my father; I did not want people to think that I was biased in any way.

I started with a history of Penikese Island and its humanitarian uses over the years. I spoke extensively about the leper colony that was there along with the dedication of the doctor, his family, and the staff. The students and parents seemed especially affected when I showed the slides of the existing gravesites and spoke of the ages of some of the patients there. Then I moved the talk into Dad's project on the island and explained his goals and hopes for the future. I even played a bit of the taped interviews of Jake and Franklin, which explained what the experiment met to them and how it has affected their lives so far.

When I was done, the room was quiet for a moment, and I wondered if I had bored them all to sleep. But then the teacher spoke up and said what a good presentation it was and opened the talk to questions. When I saw several hands shoot up, I felt better and called on one of the parents in the back of the room.

Since the writing class was at the end of the day, Mom waited for me so we could go home together. Walking out of the school, she was quiet, and I wondered what she was thinking. I felt I had done a good job and got across everything that I had planned to.

When we got in the car, she said, "Julia, I had no idea how involved you were in Dad's project, but now I see how important it is to you. You did a wonderful job presenting the facts and details about the camp while also depicting the heart and dedication an endeavor such as this needs in order to succeed. I'm so immensely proud of you, and of your dad also, of course."

After that, there was no further discussion about my summer activities as I waited anxiously to hear from Dad about his trip.

Chapter 25

Dad's fundraising trip was a big success. He not only got all the new sponsors he needed, but several of his former sponsors signed up again after they saw his new presentation. Apparently, his program was now the "future for delinquent youths," according to an article written in *The New York Times*. The article included a lot of my writings, which I was proud of. It also included a strong reference to the leper colony that had endured on Penikese for seventeen years, and it mentioned the island's spirit of helping others when things looked the most dismal. The article showed many pictures of the camp from the summer before, and I looked at them with fondness and happy memories.

When Dad called me a few days after the article was published, I congratulated him on its success. He sounded happy and excited when he started talking about the setup of the camp for the coming summer. He was expanding the program to 15 boys, and he was adding two more counselors, for a total of five. The most exciting news to me was the fact that he was going to be able to pay for three interns and two junior interns to help with the program. That meant I could be paid for my work there, which I was happy about. I felt a bit bad about not making money over the summer to help Mom and Dad with my upcoming college expenses. But the best news of all was that he had talked to Diego about taking on the other junior intern position, and Diego had agreed.

It surprised me that he would take it on considering the engineering path he was pursuing, but Dad talked him into it since he would not be able to start his job and classes until the fall. Dad went on to say that he wanted interns who were sensitive to the boys that would be at the camp and who could understand their situations. Diego fit that bill. Also, Dad explained that Diego would be helpful in the construction of the new rec center that would be built on the island during the summer.

Since I had come up with the idea for the rec center the summer before, I was proud to see it was going forward. Apparently, Dad had filed for a special grant that gave him state funding for the project. It would be underway before we got to the island, but one condition of winning the grant said that the boys would need to be involved in some way with the completion of its construction. Diego would help in organizing the crew of young men who would be supplying the added labor for the project.

I asked about Ann and Maria, and he said both would be returning. They were also hiring an assistant for Ann and a kitchen helper to assist Maria. I could not wait to talk to Diego that night. But when I called, it just went to his voicemail, so I assumed he would call me back.

When he did finally call me back a few days later, I was a bit perturbed, and some of my excitement for us to be working together had waned. He sounded tired and said he had been working extra hours at his job while finishing up his school projects. I selfishly forgot that he was a senior and that things moved much quicker at the end of the school year for them. He became quiet and then said, "My dad also won't be coming home this summer like we had planned."

Again, I had forgotten to ask him how the progress on that was going. The last we talked he was super optimistic about his dad's prospects of getting out early. He went on to explain that things were looking good after the hearing for his dad until a relative of the person who had been hurt in the robbery came forward and made a plea for no one involved to be released early. The man that had been hurt had taken a turn for the worse, and he was now on life support with things not looking good for his recovery. Though Diego's dad had not been in the building when the attack happened, the facts of the case resurfaced again, and the panel decided to put off his early release.

I told Diego that I was so sorry to hear that, and I made a note to call my dad that evening to get further details on the case. I then said, "I'm excited to see you this summer, Diego. Dad said you would be joining us at the camp after all."

He got quiet after that and just said, "Yeah, I'm not sure about that anymore, Julia. I'll have to wait and see how things shape up here and how much my stepmom needs me now that Dad won't be coming home."

When I talked to Dad later that evening, he was sad that Diego had just recently hinted he may not participate in the program. He did know about his father's recent turn of events but said that he had warned Diego and his mom that the possibility of that happening was always there. He said he would check in with Diego the following week and see how he was doing. Unfortunately, he said, he needed to have a commitment by the end of May for the position or he would have to start looking for someone else to fill it.

How can I go from so excited to so downhearted in only two days? But here I was again agonizing about the situation, with a helpless feeling that I could not shake. More and more, it seemed my constant mood swings seemed to revolve around Diego and his problems. Was that an omen for me to just get over him, or was it a sign that I was getting older and cared more for someone else rather than just myself for a change?

The last month and a half of school went by quickly, and I had little time to ponder the problem of Diego and whether he would be joining the camp. Dad had talked to him a few times, and he did say he was making progress in convincing Diego that it would be good for him to get out of the city for the summer once again. His construction job did pay more money, but Dad stressed that this intern job would look a lot better on his resume when he did apply to college. Apparently, Diego's stepmom had called Dad and told him she had been trying to encourage Diego to work at the camp also. Maybe it was time for me to put my "two cents" in, I thought to myself.

I decided to call Diego one night after our Student Awards Night, where I had just received two of the three awards I was hoping for. It was still my goal to graduate at the top of my class, and I was approaching that goal even though Dylan Daniels was giving me a run for my money. Dylan, good-naturedly, came up to me after the celebration and pointed out that we were going to get the first and second positions in the class—and that if he came in second, he was gunning for me next year. "I welcome the competition," I said as I was left the gym.

I was still thinking about that conversation with a grin when Diego answered the phone. "Hi," I said. "How have you been? Are all your classes over?"

"One more exam, and then I'm done," he answered. And then he surprised me by adding, "My stepmom is having a little graduation party for me in two weeks, if you want to come."

I did not want to hesitate with my answer, but life was a little crazy right now with the end of school. When I did not answer right away, he added, "I understand if you're too busy and you can't make it."

"I would love to, Diego, but I need to see if I can fit it in. Can you text me the exact date, time, and place?" I asked.

"Sure," he responded. "No pressure. It won't be any big thing... just a few of my friends and relatives. There's even a slight chance that my dad might be able to come for a few hours. Your father can come, too, if he'd like."

"I'll mention it to him," I said. "He said he's talked to you a few times about the camp job. Have you given it anymore thought?"

"Yes, and I'm leaning towards going. My stepmom keeps saying she'll be fine, and she did get a recent raise for one of her jobs, so things should get a little easier here. And the good thing about being at the camp, your dad pointed out, is that there is no place for us to spend the money we make, so it's all pure savings."

"I never thought of it that way," I said, "but it makes sense." I decided to put myself out there a bit, so I added quickly, "Plus, I was really looking forward to spending the summer together again."

Luckily, he did not hesitate but added, "Yeah that would be a plus also, I guess." I could hear the grin in his voice, so I accepted that as a win.

I signed off our conversation by promising to let him know about the party in a few days, and I went to bed that night with a smile on my face. I called Dad the next day and brought up the possibility of coming to the city to visit him one last time before summer started. He was excited and said that he would drop in at the party if I were going, but he would not stay too long. I worked it out with Mom that she and I would go dress shopping the following weekend for my junior prom. This time, I was going to the dance with my girlfriends and would be meeting up with other class members there.

When I mentioned that I would be going to New York the weekend after that, she hesitated before agreeing. She was worried that I was overextending myself too much. I still had two important exams left and a Spanish play to finish writing. I promised I would be able to accomplish everything in time and assured her I was not overextending myself. I think I convinced her, but I was not sure I had really convinced myself. I was feeling a bit overwhelmed with everything on my plate in addition to my never-ending goal to be the best.

Chapter 26

On the bus into New York the following weekend, I practiced reciting my Spanish play to myself and even giggled a few times at the humor I managed to insert into it. I felt comfortable enough with it to put it away and take out my class notes for my AP Calculus final. I was not quite as comfortable about that test, which I would be taking the following week, so I reviewed the notes until I surprisingly found myself in the New York bus station.

Dad met me, and we walked together to lunch. The graduation party was going to be at a hall near where Diego lived, and it would be for him and a cousin that was graduating also. I was a bit nervous about going and was glad that Dad said he would join me at the beginning at least. He would then be leaving early for an engagement with Ann. Dad explained to me that Diego's dad was denied the visit to the party at the last minute. I felt bad for Diego because I knew he was hoping he could make it. When I asked Dad why his request was turned down, he explained that it was complicated by the victim's health and that all such requests related to the people involved were being denied for the time being.

When we arrived at the event that evening, I was surprised to see that I was a bit underdressed, as I had chosen to go casual. Many of the girls were dressed up in heels and dresses, and I felt a bit out of it in my casual pants and top. There was already music playing and plenty of food was set out on platters against the wall. Diego's mom came right up to us as we entered and thanked us for coming. She led us around to introduce us to a few family members. I looked around for Diego but did not see him.

When Diego did enter with some other kids his age, he greeted everyone happily and really stood out amongst all his friends. I had forgotten how tall he was, and with all the construction work he had been doing, he had filled out even more since I had seen him last. When he did get around to seeing Dad and me, he seemed happy that we were there and grabbed my hand to go meet some of his friends. I took one last look at Dad, who just winked at me and mouthed that he was going to be leaving soon.

Diego introduced me to many of his friends he had mentioned over the past year. I bonded right away with his cousin, Emilia, who was going to NYU the following fall. I even got to meet Sophia, the girl I had been jealous of earlier in the school year. She was there with one of Diego's good friends, and they all seemed to be in a comfortable group together.

We danced and ate, and before I knew it, the club owner began flicking the lights for the end of the evening. Again, Diego and I walked part of the way back to Dad's apartment and then took the subway on the final stretch.

"I'm sorry your dad couldn't come, Diego," I said sincerely.

He just shrugged and said, "I really didn't let my hopes get up too high about it. I did have a long visit with him last week, and he is still optimistic that he may get out early. His next hearing is coming up in the fall."

Hoping to cheer him up, I handed him a small box saying, "Happy Graduation, Diego."

It was a sturdy chain with a D attached to it. "In case you forget who you are," I said with a grin. He put it on right away and seemed pleased with it.

At Dad's porch, he thanked me for coming. And before I could ask, he said, "So I'll see you in a few weeks at the camp."

"Sounds good," I said with a smile and a happy heart. Then I stood on my tippy toes and kissed him goodnight. "See you there!" I went to bed that night, counting the days until summer began and I could return to Penikese Island.

The next morning, Dad and I went out to breakfast with Ann, and then they walked me to the bus station. Dad was disappointed I could not stay for the day, but I explained to him all the work I had to accomplish before the end of the school year, and he understood. As I hugged him goodbye, I said, "See you in a couple of weeks. I can't wait to start our summer adventure."

"That's quite a different attitude than I got last summer," he said smiling.

I had planned to study on my way home on the bus, but instead I decided to close my eyes for a quick snooze. I then woke up to the sound of the bus entering the station in New Haven. *Oh well,* I thought, *so much for getting ahead of the game a little.* Mom met me at the station and started asking me about my plans for the following weekend.

"I'm not sure yet, Mom. I'll have a lot of work still to do, and I know there's a few parties I may be going to," I answered, wondering why she was so intent on knowing my every move lately.

"Sounds good," she said, "but I would like you to make sure you keep Saturday night free."

Now I was getting suspicious. My seventeenth birthday was coming up, and I hoped she was not planning on throwing me a party. I did have a big one the year before, when I turned sixteen, and though it was fun I was kind of over having a bunch of friends hanging out and discussing who was there and who was not. Last year, I had to mend a few fences when Meg and Mom made up the list to surprise me. Many of my friends, who were not particularly friendly with Meg, had been left off the list. When I asked Meg about her choices, she just said, "I invited people who care about you Julia... and friends who you should care about. Sometimes, I think you just like to pick up strays who don't fit in anywhere."

After that, I was more careful with what I shared with Meg. We had been drifting apart this year anyway, and though we were still in the same general crowd, we were not as close as we were in previous years.

Mom saw that I was lost in thought, so she hesitated before saying, "As you know, your birthday is coming up, so I thought I would invite Dad and Ann to come and join us for dinner that night."

Wow! That surprised me. I knew that Dad and Mom had been talking and that he had informed her of his relationship with Ann, but I had no idea Mom was accepting it so well. Or... was she?

"Are you sure, Mom? It's OK with me if we go out for dinner ourselves if it's going to be uncomfortable for you?"

"No, I want to meet her. And I know she means a lot to Dad... and to you," she added.

"I like her, Mom, but I don't know her all that well," I continued. "Where will they stay that evening?" Though we did have a guest room, I just couldn't picture Dad and Ann staying together in our house.

"If they're available to come then I'm sure Dad will get a hotel room for them. We'll eat in a nice restaurant downtown near where they can stay."

I wondered if she had already mentioned this to Dad. When I spoke to him the next day, he said it had come as a nice surprise and they were excited to be coming. After I hung up the phone, I suddenly had an idea that got me more excited about the upcoming dinner. Before I chickened out, I ran into Mom's office to share my idea.

"Mom, what do you think about me inviting Diego to come for my birthday dinner?" I said hopefully, "He could

126

come with Dad and Ann, and then they could drop him off afterwards."

"Oh, Hun, I'm not sure if that's such a good idea. I'm just going to be getting to know Ann, and that may be awkward for him."

"But, Mom," I pleaded, "I thought this was supposed to be my birthday dinner—not just your opportunity to become comfortable with Ann. And besides, having Diego here could be a good distraction from the awkwardness of the whole situation," I added in an exaggerated way.

"You have told me how busy he is, Julia, and you will be seeing him in a couple of weeks anyway. But if you want to ask him, go ahead and see what he says. As long as Dad and Ann are OK with bringing him," she said almost as an afterthought.

Chapter 27

Mom was probably convinced that Diego would not or could not come. But since I was on a roll, I decided to call Dad right away. He did not hesitate to say yes to the plan, but he agreed with Mom that there was a good possibility that he could not come due to all of his other obligations.

Before I called Diego, I discussed with Mom the idea that he could stay in our guest room if he came, as I was sure he could not afford to stay in the hotel where Ann and Dad would be staying. The plan was to meet them at the restaurant in town on Saturday evening and then have them come over for a birthday brunch the next morning at our house.

I called Diego on Monday evening and was surprised that he answered after a few rings. "Wow," I said nervously. "We usually play phone tag before we connect. This is unusual."

"Yeah, I'm home for a quick dinner before I head to my evening job," he answered. "What's up?"

I quickly explained to him my birthday weekend plan, and how Ann and Dad would be coming to it, and how I was wondering if he could come also, and how he could stay over at our house in the guest room and drive home with Dad and Ann the next day... And that's exactly how I said it, too—all fast and connected so I would not be interrupted with his refusal.

But he surprised me by saying, "That could work, Julia. I'll be heading to the Cape the Monday after, so I could just leave from your house rather than from here."

What?! I was so surprised and speechless when I heard his response that I did not say a word.

He then continued with, "I'm done with school, and I got some extra money from my graduation party. My mom convinced me that I should take a break and go off with a couple of my friends to the Cape before I start my summer at the camp. If it's fine with Dr. C and Ann, I'd love a ride to Connecticut and to join you guys for dinner for your birthday, Julia."

"That's great, Diego," I said quickly. "And you'll stay over at our house for brunch the next day?"

"If it's OK with your Mom, sure," he said. "I'll just need a ride to the bus station after that so I can meet up with my friends on the Cape."

I hung up in a daze, not sure how I was feeling. Suddenly, Diego seemed so much older and more sophisticated than me, and so much surer of himself. But it was a done deal now, and I needed to let my mom and dad know the plan. I had a tough school week ahead of me, but somehow, I knew the butterflies in my stomach were not there just because of that.

I did not have too much time to worry about the weekend's plans. I had two difficult finals to take along with having to present my Spanish play to the class. I had enlisted two of my friends to play the other roles the script called for, so I needed to find costumes and props for the presentation. It was supposed to be a comedy, and I hoped Senora Baker would see the humor in it.

After my first final, I rushed to the Spanish lab to set up for my play. Luckily, my two friends were there chatting, and they helped to calm down my nerves. This was my most challenging class, and I really needed to ace this final presentation in order to get the top grade I needed. I handed them their final scripts, and they quickly dressed in their costumes. I was just finishing placing the final props on the stage when the rest of the class drifted in. Behind them was our teacher, spouting directions in Spanish for us to take our seats and settle down. When she called us up to the front of the room, I felt more nervous than I thought I would—performing was not my forte at all.

But we got right into it, and the play went over surprisingly well. John, my friend from class, was a true ham and took advantage of his role as a heartbroken suitor to my self-absorbed, coquettish ingénue, who I played as the main character. The class roared through most of it, and Senora had to ask them to quiet down a few times. Now, I was worried that it was too funny and that she would not appreciate that.

At the end of the play, everyone clapped loudly, and the teacher said, "Muy buen trabajo!" I left the class satisfied that I did the best I could and headed home to study for my last final, which was scheduled for the next day.

Having survived the 'week from hell', I decided to treat myself on Friday night by accepting an invitation to a party— one that I would have ordinarily avoided. Some of my friends would be there; in fact, I was going with two of them. When Jillian picked me up that evening, Mom asked again where the party was and who would be there. I explained that it was at a senior's house and that many of my friends were going. She said as I was leaving, "Make sure you are home by midnight, Julia. We have a big day tomorrow planned. And call me if you need a ride."

I'm not sure why I went. I think I wanted to be more "grown up," like how Diego seemed to me now. After walking in, I felt out of place immediately. There was music playing, but no one was dancing. A few people were sitting around drinking, but I expected that and was not surprised. After a couple of hours of chatting with a few seniors I knew, I became quite bored and went to find my friends. They were both sitting with boys they liked, drinking and chatting away, so I walked out front to look for any other friends I knew. It appeared, however, that the few others who had been there had left. And when I went back inside, I noticed that everyone that remained was coupled up.

It was still early, but I knew I wanted to leave, so I went up to one of my friends who I came with and told her I was taking off. She just rolled her eyes and said, "Go ahead then. I'm not leaving yet. Are you going to call your mom?"

"No," I lied as I walked out of the house, not sure how I was going to get home if I didn't call my mom. Luckily, as I walked down the steps, I noticed a couple walking to their car. They were friends of mine from one of my AP classes, so I approached them and asked them for a ride home. They said it would be no problem since they were going in that direction.

When I walked into my house, my mom said, "How was your night, Hun? You're home earlier than I expected." I assured her that it was fine but that I was tired and left early. I did not tell her that the girls were still there when I left and that I had to ask for a ride home.

I went to bed that night feeling kind of alone and not sure who my friends were. I wondered if all my goals to be the best student made me odd and not fun to be around. I tried to get excited about the next day, but again I felt that Diego was so out of my league and that I was fooling myself about his feelings for me. Who was I anyway? Was I just a studious girl who did not really fit in anywhere? I went to bed feeling sorry for myself and anxious about the next day.

Chapter 28

The next morning, I did not feel much better, but I tried to build up some enthusiasm for the day. Mom was buzzing about getting an early start, and she said she had a surprise for me. She then said she had booked an appointment for us at her hair salon, where we would get both our hair and nails done. At this point, my hair was the length I liked it, though, and the color was fine now that all the brassy blonde color had grown out.

"I'm not sure, Mom. I like my hair the way it is, and my nails are fine. I did them a few weeks ago." I immediately saw the disappointment in her face, so I added quickly, "But I'll go along as long as they don't cut my hair any shorter."

She seemed pleased with that, so we set off for the day. I must admit we did have a fun time. The hairdresser trimmed my hair a bit and put some highlights in it, which I liked. We went to a store I liked, too, and Mom bought me a casual sun dress that would be perfect for the summer. We had stopped for a late breakfast, so I was hungry and excited when we finally got to the restaurant where we were meeting Dad, Ann, and Diego that evening. I was thankful to Mom for keeping me so busy throughout the day that I didn't even have a minute to get nervous about seeing him.

Dad jumped up as soon as he saw us and came over to hug me. "Happy birthday, Julia," he said. "You look beautiful!"

Ann, who had stood up to shake hands with Mom, came over to give me a hug also. "I love your hair," she said. "The highlights bring out your eyes more."

Diego stood up to meet Mom saying, "Thank you so much for inviting me to join you." Then he walked over to me and gave me a hug. "Happy birthday, Julia," he said with his adorable grin.

I felt immediately comfortable and relaxed. Mom arranged the seats so I could sit next to Diego and she could sit next to Ann. Everyone asked me about my school year, and they asked Diego about his plans now that he had graduated. He seemed proud as he told them about his job and his plans to take courses in the fall. He kept looking at me while he was talking, and I realized that he was a bit nervous. For some reason, that made me feel very protective and more grown sitting next to him.

At the end of the evening, Mom had arranged for a cake to be brought over to the table, and everyone sang to me. I did not hate the attention, and the cake was my favorite. After hugging Dad and Ann goodbye, Mom, Diego, and I headed to her car. On the way home, Diego was quiet. I realized again that he was probably nervous, so I chatted about the upcoming summer and asked him about his plans for his mini vacation on the Cape.

When we got to our house, I showed Diego his room and asked him if he wanted to come down for a soda and watch a movie with me. He seemed relieved with the idea and followed me down to the kitchen. "You have a great house," he said to my mom. "Want to watch a movie with Julia and me?"

I shot Mom a look from behind as she said, "Thanks, Diego, but I'm exhausted. I'm going to head up to bed. But you guys enjoy, and I'll see you in the morning."

After she left, we settled down in the living room with our sodas and started looking through options for movies. Before we settled on one, I asked him, "So who are you going to the Cape with?"

"Just a couple of guys I graduated with. You met one of them at my party. Do you remember Carlos? We call him Chunky, though," he said with a grin.

"I do remember him. He seemed like a lot of fun. What are your plans there? Just hanging around at the beach?" I asked, trying not to sound too curious.

"Chunky is actually starting school there in the fall. He's going to Cape Cod Community College. We're staying not far from there. He's hoping to get a job in the area, so he'll be searching for that. Plus, we'll be hanging out at the beach, of course," he said with that cute grin I tried to ignore.

"Sounds like fun," I said. "I wish I could have a break before heading off for the summer, but I still have another week of school."

We settled back to watch the latest Star Wars movie, which we had both seen before but still enjoyed. After a while he grabbed my hand, and we moved closer together. Just as he was leaning in for a kiss, we saw the light in the hallway turn on. It was Mom, of course, checking on us. "Just wanted to remind you to turn the lights off when you head up," she said. "And remember, Dad and Ann are coming over around 10 a.m. So, don't stay up too late."

Diego and I grinned at each other and watched the end of the movie, staying close together on the couch. When we stood up to head upstairs, Diego grabbed me in a hug and said, "I'm really looking forward to this summer. Are you?"

"For sure," I answered with my heart beating hard. I was afraid he could hear it, so I added quickly, "What time are you leaving tomorrow?"

"Around noonish if that works for getting a ride to the station. If not, I could always take a cab."

"I'm sure we can drop you off," I said. "You'll stay there until heading to the camp?"

"Yeah, I'll meet you and your dad at the ferry. Can you text me which one you'll be on, so I'll know which one to book?"

"Will do," I said as I stood on my tippy toes and stared at him. "Now, are you going to kiss me or not?"

We kissed for a while and then we pulled away, just looking at each other for a long time. He then reached into his pocket and pulled out a small, wrapped box.

"Happy birthday, Julia," he said.

"Thanks, Diego," I answered. "You didn't have to buy me anything."

It was a beautiful, delicate chain with the letter "D" attached to it. I looked at him and smiled. "This looks familiar."

That's when he opened the top few buttons on his shirt and there, on the chain I had given him, was the letter "J." "I figured we could switch initials—if that's OK with you?" he said hesitantly.

"It's perfect," I answered with a smile, and kissed him again. "Thank you. I love it."

I went to bed that night anxious for the summer to begin for many reasons. Suddenly, I did not feel so lonely and odd anymore. My ambitious nature was part of me, and that was not going to change. I did realize, however, that I would not be devastated if I did not make the top position in my class next year. I would continue to try my best and be satisfied with that. All my thoughts were now focused on my return to Penikese Island and the adventures I had ahead of me with the camp and Diego.

Afterword

In the 1870's, Penikese Island was the home to the Anderson Lab, the origins of the Marine Biological Laboratory that now is housed in Wood Hole, Massachusetts.

In 1905, Penikese Island was chosen to be the site of a leprosarium because it was far away from the public. At the time, leprosy, or Hansen's disease, was thought to be highly contagious, and the people who had it were considered outcasts. Now we know that it is only mildly contagious, and it is often curable with antibiotics if caught early enough.

Rough housing and a small hospital were built on the island, and a dedicated doctor and his wife agreed to take on the "experiment," as it was called then, after the initial attendant did not work out. Dr. Frank Parker and his wife, Marion, were brought on with a small staff to take care of the colonists. They stayed committed to the cause until the colony closed in 1921. The colony grew over time and had a total of thirty-six patients. Fourteen of them died while they were there, and they are buried on the site.

Besides food and housing, the residents had access to medical attention, religious services, education, leisure activities, and work on the island. Oftentimes, they would do light farming or landscaping, which was all supervised by Dr. Parker and his wife. To build up their self-esteem, Dr. Parker gave the patients paid jobs so they could order personal items from stores in New Bedford. To protect their dignity, he discouraged passing ships from gawking or taking photographs. Marion equipped the patients with radios, record players, books, and magazines as well.

One sixteen-year-old resident, Archie Thomas, who arrived in 1912, received a two-way radio and began communicating with operators on other islands as well as those on passing ships. He provided the residents with their only contact to the outside world, and when he died in 1915, much of the communication slowed down since no one else knew how to use his equipment.

In 1921, a large federal hospital was built in Louisiana. Over Dr. Parker's objections, the governor of Massachusetts ordered the colony on Penikese to be shut down and for all the sixteen remaining residents to be moved to the new facility. The existing buildings from the site were ordered to be burnt down and then imploded with dynamite to prevent the spread of the disease. Because Dr. Parker had complained about the medical profession and their lack of sympathy and empathy toward leprosy, he was shunned by the State of Massachusetts, his pension was cut off, and he and Marion were forced to move to Montana to live with their son.

From 1973 to 2011, the island housed The Penikese Island School for troubled boys, most of whom were recovering from opiate or alcohol addiction. The camp has been referred to as a boot camp where the boys constructed the dormitories and classrooms, raised food, cut wood, and were expected to incorporate the values of the mentors there. Unfortunately, when many of them returned to the mainland, they returned to their life of crime. Still, sixteen percent of them kept out of trouble, found work, and did well. The project ended when the founder, George Cadwalader, became discouraged and gave up on the endeavor after state funding ceased.

Today, the island is a wildlife sanctuary, and it is open to tourists and school children by appointment.

CPSIA information can be obtained
at www.ICGtesting.com
Printed in the USA
LVHW031432070521
686792LV00003B/191